CVC
8

CVC

Carter V. Cooper

SHORT FICTION ANTHOLOGY SERIES

BOOK EIGHT

SELECTED BY AND WITH A PREFACE BY

Gloria Vanderbilt

EXILE
editions
Fiction, Poetry, Translation, Drama and Nonfiction

Carter V. Cooper Short Fiction Anthology Series, Book Eight.
Issued in print and electronic formats.

ISSN 2371-3968 (Print)
ISSN 2371-3976 (Online)

ISBN 978-1-55096-845-3 (paperback). ISBN 978-1-55096-846-0 (epub).
ISBN 978-1-55096-847-7 (kindle). ISBN 978-1-55096-848-4 (pdf).

Short stories, Canadian (English). Canadian fiction (English) 21st century.
Vanderbilt, Gloria, 1924-, editor. Series: Carter V. Cooper short fiction anthology
series, book 8.

Published by Exile Editions Limited. ExileEditions.com
144483 Southgate Road 14 – GD, Holstein, Ontario, N0G 2A0
Printed and Bound in Canada in 2019, by Marquis

We gratefully acknowledge, for their support toward our publishing activities,
the Canada Council for the Arts, the Government of Canada,
the Ontario Arts Council, and the Ontario Media Development Corporation.

Canadian sales: The Canadian Manda Group, 664 Annette Street,
Toronto ON M6S 2C8 www.mandagroup.com 416 516 0911

North American and international distribution, and U.S. sales:
Independent Publishers Group, 814 North Franklin Street,
Chicago IL 60610 www.ipgbook.com toll free: 1 800 888 4741

In memory of

Carter V. Cooper

The Winners for Year Eight

Best Story by an Emerging Writer

∽ $10,000 ∽

Leanne Milech

Best Story by a Writer at Any Point of Career
(judged as equal in merit – sharing the prize)

∽ $2,500 ∽

Edward Brown

∽ $2,500 ∽

Priscila Uppal

CVC
BOOK EIGHT

PREFACE

I founded the Carter V. Cooper short fiction competition in memory of my son, and to champion literature, which he had loved.

It is one of the great joys of parenthood to behold, in astonishment and surprise, the depth and complexity of your children as they emerge into themselves. In that spirit, I cannot help but admire the writers who comprise *Book Eight* of the *Carter V. Cooper Short Fiction Anthology Series*.

Open to all Canadian writers, this annual short fiction competition awards two prizes: $10,000 for the best story by an emerging writer, and $5,000 for the best story by an established writer.

Believing, as I have said before, that all writing is born of a singular yearning to see a truth with one's own eyes, these eleven stories – in genre, range, tone, and interest – are all utterly their own.

During the latter part of the 2018 summer – and then final deliberations through September into October – our judges spent untold hours reading and assessing and discussing many hundreds of submissions to this year's competition.

They tell me that they were very impressed by the technical prowess, dexterity of language, and diversity of writers and voices represented in the stories. And, once they arrived at a short list, I was delighted to see such a wide variety of themes and settings in those stories.

About the winners, I have this to say: "The Light in the Closet" by Leanne Milech is the winner in the Emerging Writer category. It is a family story told with verve and wit, touching on the psychotic without becoming grotesque, the ludicrous without becoming laughable, and ends with a moment of pathos that is not pathetic.

I agree with the judges that the Established and/or At Any Career Point award is to be split between two stories: "Remember Me" by Edward Brown and "Elevator Shoes" by Priscila Uppal. Each story is set in a different century, and each possesses its own unique voice. Both evoke a strong sense of place from their opening sentences, and their narratives play out effortlessly in the mind's eye – the historical drama of a nineteenth-century Toronto gaol hanging and its aftermath, and a breezy contemporary telenovela episode about a woman and her beloved shoes.

I am once again proud and thrilled that all these wonderful writers are to be presented in the annual *Carter V. Cooper Short Fiction Anthology Series* – as always, a special edition published in memory of my beloved son, Carter, who is no longer with us, but remains in spirit through this competition, these books, and all of your wonderful writing!

With great gratitude I thank the readers who adjudicated this competition: Randall Perry, Matt Shaw, Dani Spinosa, and Jerry Tutunjian…all who have played their own special roles in the development and support of emerging writers.

Gloria Vanderbilt

Gloria Vanderbilt
February 2019

Leanne Milech

THE LIGHT
IN THE CLOSET

I

My dad, Marty, was a Jewish boy from Montreal. He was based in Calgary and posing as a cowboy when he first heard about my mother. His ex-girlfriend had written from Toronto to tell him she'd just met Claudia, this foxy Jewish chick he would love because she had really big boobs. It's hard to believe that a woman would write a letter like that to her ex-boyfriend, but my dad always swore that it was true.

He was a twenty-nine-year-old travelling souvenir salesman when he got the letter. By then, he'd driven across Canada and swerved off a cliff in British Columbia's Rocky Mountains, miraculously surviving with only a bruise. The night before the accident, my dad had given himself to Jesus down on a hotel room floor after watching a local evangelical talk show on TV. That moment was just one of his many flirtations with different religions – he didn't become a devout Christian after the car crash even though it seemed like Jesus had saved his life. My father liked having lots of different religious tricks in his toolbox because he always seemed to need them and different ones worked at different times. Also, Marty loved a freebie. Loyalty was irrelevant. He mooched off whichever religion seemed like the shiniest new toy.

When my father met my mother, she seemed pretty sparkly. She was thirty-one and living in Toronto in a new high-rise apartment building. She was an office temp with income supplemented by her father, David. There was no other way that she could have afforded such a swanky place – it had two bedrooms, two bathrooms, and brand-new appliances.

My dad knocked on my mother's door for their first date wearing a cowboy hat, shearling coat, and cowboy boots. My mother's boobs answered the door first. My dad took his hat off and held it to his chest. She said, Good, leave it off, you look like a *goy* in that outfit. He said she looked good in the light of the hall. She was curvy and short and had a beauty mark underneath her lip. Then he shook her hand and then they kissed and then they had sex and then my mother told my father that she wanted to marry him. It was a fast little romance, but that's the way my mother rolled. She was quick to commit.

There'd been two husbands before my dad.

First, there was Jersey the Diabetic, who, battling depression after being diagnosed with diabetes, put a steak knife through his stomach while my mother was out shopping one day. While Jersey was in the hospital recovering, David moved my mother and all the furniture he'd paid for out of their house. When Jersey staggered back home, all he found were lonely dust bunnies and his clothes hanging themselves in the closet.

Then there was Henry the Rabbi, who became Orthodox soon after my mother married him. One day, Henry went to Florida and grew a long beard and never came back.

Given my mother's luck with love, her parents must have been happy that there was another potential husband when she told them about my dad. But when my mother asked to move to Calgary to be with him, David said, Over my dead body.

My dad didn't question the fact that a thirty-one-year-old woman couldn't move to a different city because her father wouldn't allow it. He just put his cowboy hat back on, packed up his life in Calgary, and came back to Toronto wearing jeans and a T-shirt, ready for marriage.

My mother's money wasn't the only reason my dad married her. Before the letter from his ex-girlfriend had arrived, my dad was walking down a path to the souvenir shop at the Calgary Zoo when he saw them: a girl of about three, resting her chin on her dad's head while he held her feet. They passed my dad by in an instant that changed his life. That's when he knew, more than anything else, that he wanted to be a father.

After he moved, my dad tried to sell souvenirs in Toronto, but he wasn't successful. He complained to a nice young guy who owned a souvenir shop. He was worried that moving to Toronto had been a mistake. The guy pointed to the sky and said that my dad shouldn't second-guess himself because God always works things out. He was as convincing as the televangelist in the hotel room that had sold my dad on the idea of devoting himself to Jesus for a night.

When he lost his job, my dad took the souvenir guy's words as clues to stay put, and he settled into life with my mother. It wasn't a very hard life since David gave my mother plenty of money to live on while she temped.

After my dad had moved in with my mother, but before they were married, he saw a bottle of pills on the coffee table. He asked my mother what they were for. She said they were special prescription vitamins, and he believed her.

My dad's sister, Libby, didn't. She'd tried to tell my dad that something about my mother was off. Libby had gotten a bad vibe from my mother because the hem of her skirt had been undone on one side the first time they'd met. That doesn't

15

mean anything, my dad told Libby when she shared her suspicions.

I wonder now if there was a thread loose on my mother's wedding dress, too.

As a child, my mother had skipped a grade and played beautiful piano. No one could have predicted the future, that my mother would first be hospitalized for depression when she was just twelve years old. That she would be in and out of the hospital for the rest of her life.

My mother stopped taking her antidepressants when she was pregnant with me. When I was two months old, she sauntered into the living room and told my father that her cousin, Linda, was talking to her through the radio. There was a new diagnosis that day. My mother was paranoid schizophrenic now.

My father stayed with my mother after she was diagnosed. They'd had a baby. And a girl needs her mother. But it was my father who made my formula. It was too difficult for my mother, whose hands shook from her medication. After I was off formula, my dad tried to work here and there. He held down a few different telemarketing sales jobs for a month at a time. But it was hard for him to focus at work. My mother got sick every six months or so. Sometimes she stopped taking her pills. Sometimes they stopped working. My dad never knew exactly when her next breakdown would happen. What if my mother got confused and left me in the bathtub by myself? What if she went for a walk and forgot to come back? She couldn't exactly be alone with me, so my dad had stopped trying to work at all by the time I was three. He didn't need to work anyway. David gave my parents money from GICs and the apartment buildings he bought and sold. He bought us a small brick bungalow on Ruby Avenue. We called the house Ruby, like it was a treasure.

When I was very young, my parents threw lavish brunches for family and friends at Ruby. Back then, my mother still had friends. My parents spread out giant platters of bagels, lox, and cream cheese. My mother wore outfits with matching tops and skirts. I had great big cakes. People clapped while I blew out the candles and turned two, three, four, five.

Since they didn't work, my parents passed a lot of time spending David's money. When I was two, we went to the Bahamas where I ate escargot and ran around our hotel's casino while my dad gambled. I went under the betting tables and popped the ashtrays out from their corner slots. We flew to Florida when I was in kindergarten. When we went deep-sea fishing, my dad wore a little blue hat that said "CAPTAIN" in gold letters. We bought a Hollywood condo before we left, but then quickly sold it.

In Toronto, we went out to restaurants. We often went shopping. My parents bought abstract art, kitchen appliances, and gourmet food. We went to Toys "R" Us regularly. We got our hair done. I didn't have a bedtime, and we ate at all hours of the day. Even if I'd had dinner, at nine o'clock at night, I could order a hamburger from my dad, and he would go to the kitchen and fry it up for me. I could have anything I wanted, whenever I wanted it.

I could even choose whether or not to go to school. I'd gone to Hebrew school in kindergarten and hadn't minded it, but in Grade One, my teachers were strict. I started many mornings by skipping to the end of Ruby's driveway, looking up at the Russian bus driver, Boris, telling his moustache that I wasn't going to school that day, and skipping back inside.

One morning after I'd waved Boris away, I wandered around looking for my dad. He wasn't in my parents' nicotine-yellow bedroom, but my mother was. She was lying in bed. We called my parents' king-size bed "The Big Bed." By then, my mother had

17

begun spending a lot of time in The Big Bed. Usually, she slept in The Big Bed by herself. My dad liked sleeping with me. We cuddled in our underwear. He felt so cozy. He was my favourite stuffed animal.

My mother just lay in The Big Bed, the window shades drawn and the sheets half-off. She'd chew bubble gum and stick the used, slobbery pieces onto the side of her night table where they dried up into a gross but beautiful rainbow. She wore her makeup face in The Big Bed. Lipstick outside the lines of her lips. Stained teeth. She read Danielle Steel and Sidney Sheldon in The Big Bed. She ate cottage cheese and smoked.

When she wanted to watch television, she went to the living room. She spent almost every afternoon watching "The Young and the Restless" and "The Bold and the Beautiful" while my dad read Timothy Leary and Ram Dass on the couch next to her. If I was playing hooky from school, I sat on the floor at their feet, writing stories about pretty, perfect girls who wore strawberry-flavoured lip gloss. I thought I might be cute because sometimes strangers asked me if I was the actress who played Punky Brewster on TV, but I knew, deep in my bones, that I wasn't pretty or perfect. All I had to do was look at my mother to be able to see that.

If we got bored of the living room, my dad and I sometimes danced around my room, my arms around his neck, my legs wrapped around his waist. Sometimes, I'd gaze into his small red eyes and say, Daddy, why are you being so extra fun today?

Sometimes my dad and I went on dates. We went to the mall, the bookstore, the library, and the movies. The movies were the best because when the lights went out, no one knew where we were. Not even my mother.

Since he didn't have a job, my dad spent a lot of time looking for God. And since I was often home from school in Grade One, I looked with him. My dad didn't feel very connected to Judaism, so we didn't go to synagogue. We went to ashrams. We went to the Unity Church of Truth. We went to *satsangs*. I remember sitting cross-legged on the floor of a meditation hall. Everyone around us said *om om om om mani padme hum*. The tall man on the stage with the yellow robes patted my head and said I was a good little girl. Then at home my dad took a bath and droned *om mani padme hum* under a special light bulb that flooded the bathroom red.

We even looked for God at motivational seminars. My dad took me and my mother to the Bob Proctor seminar at York University. It was called "Born Rich." We sat in an auditorium while Bob Proctor lectured on the stage, strolling back and forth. I followed him with my eyes while my mother snored and my father wrote "Come Spirit of God" in a workbook next to Bob Proctor's typed message. The message said, "Spirit can only express itself through the medium of an acorn in accordance with the limitations placed on the acorn; and the medium of the acorn is limited by the 'patterned plan' or the 'nucleus of the seed.'"

My mother was a hard little seed in the pit of my stomach. I looked over at her while she slept in her chair. She was too big. She made my stomach hurt. That's why I usually wailed, Leave Jabba the Hutt at home, *pleeeeeease* whenever my dad suggested that she go on an adventure with us. He often listened to me and told her to stay home.

I switched schools when I was seven. At the end of Grade One, my English teacher called my dad and told him he was a delinquent parent, so I went to an arts public school near Ruby for Grade Two. My new friends and I acted out scenes from *Ghostbusters* at recess. I pretended to be Sigourney Weaver.

My teacher was Kathy Glass. She read us stories while we sat on the carpet. I closed my eyes while I listened. Her voice could lull me to sleep.

Sometimes my dad woke me up in the middle of the night to play Nintendo. Daddy, I have school, I'd say, throaty with sleep, eyes closed. He'd turn the light on and say, Shhh, don't wake Jabba. I tumbled out of bed and followed him into the living room and played for an hour or two. If he did better than me, I karate-chopped him and kicked him in the chest and we fell over laughing. Then we played some more until I passed out and morning came.

Only one thing truly bothered me. I knew there was something wrong with my mother. I don't remember any of her breakdowns before I turned seven. I just knew, as if I'd always known, that something was very wrong with her. It was her hands that gave her away. They were so shaky, and her nails were so long and bumpy and red. I often ripped my own hands away if she tried to hold them. I skulked around the grocery store, afraid that everyone could see how shaky my mother's hands were. I watched other mothers wheel down the aisles in straight lines. I held onto my father's legs so they knew which parent I really belonged to.

What was wrong with her exactly?

I didn't know.

I just knew that my dad and I sometimes played pretend. We pretended it was normal for my mother to stay up all night, talking to the kitchen sink or giggling into a radio antenna. I knew she took pills. I knew that sometimes they stopped working or she stopped taking them. I knew that to get her into the hospital against her will, we had to prove she was *adangertoherselforothers*.

Nobody explained these things to me when I turned seven. I don't know how I knew them. I just did.

When I was growing up, my dad sometimes went to visit a man named Justice of the Peace. He'd come back with a piece of paper called a Form 1. Then he'd call the cops and they'd take my mother to the hospital. But sometimes we coaxed her into the car on our own, saying we were just going for a little drive. Then we'd take her to the hospital and try to convince the doctors to admit her. If we brought her to the hospital when she wasn't sick enough, they'd turn us away.

Whenever this happened, it made me feel hopeless and sad. During those car rides back to Ruby while she talked to herself, it didn't matter that I went on vacations and ate in restaurants all the time. It didn't matter that I looked a little like Punky Brewster. It didn't even matter that I had a super-fun dad. Those car rides made me feel so lonely, as if the world didn't care about what happened to us and probably never would.

II

Who are you dancing with, Mom?

Pierre Trudeau, she said, swaying.

I sat on the floor, watching, seven years old, tangled up in our white curtains, sucking my thumb. My mother had been dancing with Pierre Trudeau in the living room for a few days, whirling around to her Righteous Brothers record. She wore her favourite nightgown. It was long and grey, sleeveless and satin. She didn't wear a bra, so her nipples poked through. Her breasts hung down, sloppy. She spun. Pierre, she crooned, her eyes closed. Her arms up around Pierre's invisible neck, she sang along to "You've Lost That Lovin' Feelin'," off-key.

I pulled the curtains in front of my face and closed my eyes.

I knew that imagining a prime minister as her dance partner didn't make my mother *adangertoherselforothers*. My dad and I were pretending that everything was normal until she tried to do something truly crazy, like burn Ruby down. Since we were pretending everything was okay, I invited a new friend from school, Tabitha, to come over and play Nintendo.

Tabitha and I sat super-close to the TV, our eyes glued to the little Luigi and Mario figures, the tiny yellow mushrooms and the bright blue electronic sky. The TV's static made strands of Tabitha's thin, light brown hair fly off her head. While she played, I watched her hair float.

My parents were in the kitchen making hamburgers. I heard them fighting and turned the volume up on the TV.

Claudia, I told you not to use the breadcrumbs. What are you doing?

Shut up you bastard.

Silence.

Shuffling on the floor.

Dad mumbling.

Then, my mother: Oh yeah? Fuck you, fuck your sister, and *fuck* her deformed baby.

I flinched. Aunt Libby had just given birth to a baby with a cleft lip.

Tabitha looked at me. Your turn, she said. She chewed her bottom lip with her buck tooth. She glanced around the room. I think my mom's going to be here soon.

Great, I said, concentrating on shooting fireballs at flying turtles.

The slap from the kitchen was loud enough for us to hear. Hard and fast. Tabitha stood. I kept playing. I heard the plastic container fall over on the counter, the breadcrumbs spilling onto the floor, as loud as a waterfall. My mother ran to The Big Bed and slammed the bedroom door. Tabitha started to cry.

Don't cry, I hissed at her. Baby, I thought. But I had a lump in my throat the size of a whole hamburger. I sat up on my knees and dug them into the carpet. While my knees burned, I prayed that Tabitha's mother would show up. A few minutes later, our doorbell rang. I practically shoved Tabitha out the door while she put on her winter boots. Her mother grabbed her by the head and turned her around, leading Tabitha down the cement steps. Tabitha's mother had a huge bum. I stared at it as they walked away. I wondered if Tabitha would grow up to be like her mother or if I'd be like mine one day. The thought terrified me.

In the kitchen, raw hamburger meat sat on a broiling pan. A pot boiled, broccoli drowning inside. I stepped over the breadcrumbs and tapped my dad on the shoulder. He was sitting at the kitchen table with his head down.

Daddy, the broccoli's ready, I said.

She's cracking up again, Em, he said.

In my head, I said "starting now" over and over again. "Starting now" was my private incantation. I used it whenever I wanted to begin my life anew. As soon as I said "starting now," everything would be perfect, including me. I would be pretty and smart. My mother wouldn't listen to The Righteous Brothers anymore. She'd take the silver nightgown off and put on a matching top and skirt. And my father would never smack her again.

Later that night, I woke up to red swirling lights and two cops in the front hall. The lady cop tried to pick me up and hold me, but I batted her arm away and looked around wildly for my dad. He was in the living room on the flower-print couch. The flowers were as white as the whites of the lady cop's eyes, who was kneeling down now, staring at my face. I felt like swatting the tip of her nose.

She's sick, my dad said to the cop standing over him.

The cop wrote some notes on a pad of paper. Sick with what?

My dad said, Paranoid schizophrenia. The cop scribbled. It was the first time I'd heard those words. "Paranoid Schizophrenia" sounded like the name of a monster.

I ran to my parents' room. My mother was sitting on the edge of The Big Bed calmly smoking a cigarette.

What happened?

Daddy hit me and now he's going to jail. Bastard.

I ran back down the hall. My heart jumped up and down in its cage. The lady cop blocked the doorway to the living room. I tried to push past her, tried crawling around her.

Daddy, I yelled. The lady cop picked me up then and put my hair behind my ear. Her fingers were cold like the handcuffs around my dad's wrists.

The lady cop turned me around so I couldn't see the other cop and my dad as they brushed past us. She put me down and followed them out the door. I chased them. The screen door closed in my face. The cops took my dad down the steps, one on each side of him. I mashed my face into the screen's tiny squares. I listened to the cops' boots crunching snow. Blades of grass stuck up through our white lawn. I watched the cops shove my dad into the backseat of their car. I watched them get into the front. I watched their silent red lights spin.

My mother came up behind me, smoky and slow. She touched the back of my neck. I turned around. Her satin nightgown was ripped at the bottom. I sniffled as she showed me her arm. The red spot was shaped like an awkward star. She pointed and said, Look at what your daddy did. I pressed against the screen. I asked when Daddy was coming home. My mother laughed and walked away. Lit a cigarette on the burner in the kitchen. Asked if I was hungry. Then she talked silently to the voices in her head. I watched her mouth move for a while before I got too tired and went to my room to sleep.

I couldn't fall asleep in my own bed, so, eventually, I crawled into The Big Bed. My parents' room was like a cave. Very dark. The sheets on The Big Bed felt sandy. I didn't like it in there. The Big Bed was brown and wooden. It had an elaborately carved headboard with bumps and grooves that could be hills or islands or fairy-tale castles. I lay on my back and twisted my hand behind me so I could touch the headboard. I was looking for a tiny British worm like the one in my favourite movie, *Labyrinth*. In the movie, the worm tells a teenage girl searching for her kidnapped baby brother which way to go. I wanted some directions too.

My mother slept beside me on her back, snoring. The radio sat blaring on the chewing gum night table. My mother needed the radio to be loud. That way, she could hear the voices meant just for her: her dead mother, her cousin.

I thought things over and decided that, by morning, my dad would be home again. He would save me, like the Jesus they talked about at Unity Church. I pictured my dad driving up to Ruby looking exactly like Jesus, his hair all long and blowing out the window. Now that I thought about it, my dad could basically be Jesus' twin. They had similar mouths. How could I have not realized that before? Of course! The next morning my dad would arrive, wearing a big cross around his neck, telling me this had all been a bad joke. Some upside-down trick from heaven. He'd say that I didn't have to be alone with my mother. Or my dad would be at school in the morning, holding the door to my classroom open. In fact, Ms. Glass was probably already making arrangements with him for the next day.

I had almost fallen asleep dreaming about school when the phone on the night table rang. I reached over and grabbed it.

Hello?

Hello. Is this Mrs. Bloom?

No. This is Emily.

Well, hi, Emily. How are you doing?

Who is this? My elbow dug into my mother's stomach, the receiver to my ear. She didn't wake up.

I'm calling from Toronto Police Services. Just checking in to make sure everything is all right over there.

When is my daddy coming home? My voice was loud enough for the lady cop to hear, but not loud enough to wake my mother.

The lady cop said she didn't know. She said, You have to be A Big Girl now.

I really wanted to say, But I can't be A Big Girl now, I'm stuck with a crazy woman, she is *adangertoherselforothers*, I need help! But I couldn't get the words out. Instead, I hung up the phone. I rolled off my mother and onto my back, shifting as far away from her as I could. I said "starting now" and stared up at the ceiling. The ceiling had smoke stains on it. Imperfectly shaped yellow circles. I imagined that they were clouds or teapots. For a split second, I even thought I saw God. He looked like a yellow pool of light. But then I blinked and He was just a circle of nicotine again.

I woke up on my side with my head in my mother's neck, my arms wrapped around her waist. I unclasped my hands and crawled to the end of the bed. My arms felt like they had bugs crawling all over them.

My mother was still sleeping, her stomach rising and falling in early morning light. My bangs were sticking up. I sat on the edge of the bed and sucked my thumb until she opened her eyes.

We didn't have breakfast, but my mother drove me to school. My school was close to Ruby, but that drive took forever. The circles under my mother's eyes were darker than usual. Whenever she turned the wheel, her upper arm jiggled. She was still wearing the nightgown. I gripped my door and stared at the houses we passed, thinking about the people inside. The little girls with silky blond ponytails. The mothers who brushed their hair. The fathers who kissed them goodbye.

The second we arrived at school, I bolted out of the car like it was about to explode.

Ms. Glass stood at the door to my classroom wearing a navy dress and red-framed glasses. She looked especially kind and smart that day. But instead of scooping me up, kissing me on the cheek and whispering that my dad was there, she just said, Good morning, Emily.

Good morning, Ms. Glass, I said, looking down. If I looked into her eyes, I'd cry so hard that I wouldn't be able to stop.

My class was working on our art projects. My friend Samantha and I sat at two desks facing each other. Our desks were next to a window overlooking the playground and the street. I looked at the spot where my dad usually picked me up from school. I was afraid that my mother would be sitting there in the car, that she'd wait for me all day, waving to me through the windshield. She wasn't there, though. Then I became worried that she'd forget to pick me up. I'd get lost walking home, fall asleep in a snowbank somewhere and wake up half-frozen the next morning.

I shuddered, looked down and casually brushed blobs of paint onto my paper.

What are you making? Samantha looked at my picture, tilting her head.

It's abstract.

What's that mean?

I don't know, I said. My dad likes abstract art. I'm making him a picture.

Oh, Samantha said. She went back to her painting.

I dipped my brush in a cup of water. My dad got arrested last night, I said suddenly, looking up. The words just fell out of me. I doubted Samantha would understand, but it was worth a try.

She practically lost her mind. You mean, like, he's in jail? Her blue eyes were circles. Yep, I said, trying to be cool about it. It's a mistake, though. He's coming to pick me up after school.

The way she looked at me, I felt like Mary Tulle must have felt in gym when we were doing Israeli folk dancing and her underwear fell off in the middle of the floor. I looked from Samantha's round blue eyes to her straight blond hair. I wished I'd just kept my mouth shut and painted a rainbow and some bunnies.

When the bell rang at the end of the day, I struggled into my coat and shoved my hands into my pockets. I had that nervous feeling I got whenever I knew I was about to do something really hard, like have a tooth pulled or get a booster shot. As I neared the classroom door, I turned to look at Ms. Glass. She was sitting at her desk. I felt like trotting up to her and burying my face in her lap. I wanted her to kiss my neck. I wanted to sob into her body and tell her that my mother was crazy. Take me home with you, I wanted to wail. But I was too afraid and shy to say any of these things. Instead, I left the room.

I looked out the window as I made my way down the stairs. I saw our car. My mother's dark figure was behind the wheel, waiting. I took a deep breath. I opened the door and joined her.

We're going to Swiss Chalet for dinner, my mother said. She drove a little too fast. She talked to Pierre a bit. Well, of course Justin is handsome. Look at his father. No, honey, neither of them is as handsome as you. You know that. She tapped the wheel playfully and threw her head back, laughing. When she wasn't talking to herself, she called the other drivers dirty words. I let a long breath out when we pulled up to the man in the parking lot booth at the restaurant. We'd made it. My stomach growled in anticipation of food – chicken falling off the bone, French fries dripping in special sauce and ketchup.

The parking lot attendant had dark skin and a thin, drooping moustache. He slid his window open and stuck his head out. My mother rolled her window down. I hoped she wouldn't say anything too strange. The man gave her a ticket and told her to turn left to the garage door entrance. She took the ticket and whipped the car around. The garage door didn't open. She turned the car off. The door still didn't budge. A couple of cars were lined up behind us now. Snow shot out of the darkening sky. My nose was getting cold.

Mom, start the car.

Her eyes flashed the way a light bulb does just before it burns itself out. The cars behind us honked. I curled into myself. I willed that garage door open, prayed to God down on my knees in my head. Said I'd be the best girl in the world if it opened. Still, it didn't move. Not an inch.

She turned the car on again as the person behind us rolled down his window and shouted at us to move. I sank low in my seat. My mother screeched around the semi-circle of driveway until she was back at the dark-skinned man's booth. I got on my knees and looked out the back window. I watched the door creak up for the first car and stay open for the second. Both cars sailed in, smooth and magical.

There are no fucking spots in there, my mother told the man, waving her ticket in his face.

Ma'am, there are plenty of spaces. Those cars just went in. The man gestured behind him with his thumb.

She said, There. Are. No. Fucking. Spaces. I felt heat rising from her skin.

That will be five dollars, ma'am.

For what? She was screaming now.

Flat rate, ma'am.

She threw the ticket in his face, rolled up her window and drove us backwards into the street. As she took us home, she muttered something about the fucking Pakis taking over every goddamn fucking thing.

My mother sat at the kitchen table for the rest of the night, cutting up family photos. Stacks of albums lined the table, their covers sticky with old food and melted candle wax. I sat at the table, not knowing what else to do. I watched my mother shred people. She cut my dad out of a picture of us in Florida. I was wearing Mickey Mouse ears, and he had his arm around me. We smiled big for the camera. Now his head was just a crooked circle on the table that I picked out of the pile of scraps and held in my hand.

I kept thinking that someone would come for me: Ms. Glass, the lady cop, anyone. But eventually, I believed no one was coming for me at all. So when Ms. Glass took me down to the office at recess a week later and my dad was sitting on my principal's couch, I didn't believe he was real. The couch was in front of a window, and soft grey light filtered in from outside, illuminating his hair, his face. He was drinking a cup of coffee and wearing his cuddly grey ski sweater. He looked good, like a teddy bear. He smiled and his eyes got all small, like they always did, so small that they pretty much disappeared. I stood at the door, shy, not sure if he was there to stay.

We took a taxi to a low brick building. The sign outside said you could rent furnished apartments, short or long term. The lady at the welcome desk had blond hair done in tight curls that cascaded down her back, like a movie star or a mermaid. She was beautiful.

My dad and I asked about a room. A cat crept out from behind the counter and rubbed up against my leg. The Mermaid's eyes sparkled. My dad said he really had a thing for cats and hoped to have some purebreds one day, Himalayans, or maybe Persians. The Mermaid said she loved both those breeds and that she had a room for us. As she led us down the hall, I thought about what would happen if my mother went to school to pick me up and I wasn't there. She would probably yell and swear at Ms. Glass in the halls. I felt embarrassed and pushed the thought away.

The room had thin walls covered in old flowered wallpaper and twin beds with tough, springy mattresses perfect for jumping. As soon as I saw them, I started leaping from one to the other like they were trampolines. The Mermaid leaned on the doorframe and watched me. I tried to show off a little, but I didn't know how to do anything special so I just made loud yelps every time I landed on a bed and hoped that would entertain her. My dad asked her what she was doing for dinner. She said she was busy.

When she left, I flopped onto my back and felt a little bit empty. The Mermaid didn't want to go on a date with us, and I felt just as rejected as if I'd asked her out myself. I'd thought that as soon as my dad and I were alone, a new mother would be waiting for me in the wings, ready to join us with open arms.

But there was a horrible blackness surrounding us, and ever since That Night, I'd known its name: schizophrenia. The Mermaid could smell the schizophrenia on us. She could see it and feel it. We were marked, just like my mother.

III

When I woke up in the morning, my dad already had his coat on. He was tapping his thumb and forefinger together over and over again.

I rubbed my eyes and sat up. Daddy, where are we going?

We're going home, Emily. This is totally nuts. If we don't go back, Jabba will be a bag lady.

I pictured my mother with a shopping cart full of broken lamps and glass bottles, wheeling away downtown, swearing at people and laughing and two-stepping with Pierre on the sidewalk.

My dad got up and started pacing. Plus, we don't have any money.

You could get a job, I said.

But then who would take care of you? Put your coat on.

I looked around the room frantically, hoping the Mermaid would magically appear and convince my dad to stay.

We can't go back, Daddy, please.

My dad held out my coat. The light fixture above his head flickered. I looked at him for a long time. Now that I thought about it, he didn't look like Jesus at all.

Back at Ruby, my mother roamed up and down the hallway for a few days. She stayed up all night. She lit cigarettes on the stove and walked back to her room, crushing them out on her night table. But she gradually got better on her own. Sometimes that happened. She would start taking her pills again for some reason and return to her version of normal.

She watched "The Young and the Restless" and went for walks around the block. She got her hair done. She stopped talking to herself and listening to the radio for messages from dead people. My dad pretended like That Night, his time in jail, and our brief sleepover at the Mermaid's had never happened.

I pretended to be Nancy Drew whenever my mother got better. I was constantly looking for signs that her normal was beginning to unravel. Eventually, it always did.

About six months after we got home from the Mermaid's, my dad and I sat at the kitchen table eating breakfast. My dad was reading the paper and chuckling at a comic strip. I was buttering toast and inspecting my mother as she washed dishes.

When I saw her whispering into the dish soap, I elbowed my dad.

She's talking to herself again, I hissed.

My dad looked over at my mother. Then he looked at me.

I don't see anything, he said. Everything's going to be okay now. You gotta relax.

He put his hand on mine. It felt cold. Then he went back to the comics.

Soon after that, my dad stopped sleeping in my bed with me. He stopped looking for God, too. No more *satsangs*, no more Unity Church. He smoked the cigarettes that made his eyes go red. I didn't find him nearly as fun anymore, but I still missed him. It was lonely in my room with nobody to cuddle.

One night, a few months later, I found myself roaming around the basement looking for a couple of things. First, I was desperate to find God – my dad could give up, but that didn't mean I had to give up, too. Second, I wanted to find an old stuffed toy, the one I'd loved when I was six. He was a snuggly brown squirrel with a bushy tail and an acorn-print bandana around his neck.

I looked in a bunch of boxes filled with toys. I sifted through My Little Ponys, stopping to stroke their knotted hair. I ran my hands along the bodies of naked Barbie dolls. But the squirrel was nowhere to be found. God was playing a good game of hide-and-seek, too. I decided to check the laundry room. One of them had to be in there.

As soon as I walked in, I noticed a door I'd never seen before. My dad had finally gotten rid of the old black bookcase with the loose back panel and the lopsided shelves. There was a door in the wall that had been hidden by the bookcase. It had a shiny golden handle. Maybe God was in there.

I opened the door and discovered an old closet. It was stuffed with puffy parkas and long leather coats. I saw a shearling coat that I wanted to pull on top of me like a blanket. I pushed my way inside the closet and closed the door. I waded to the back corner of the closet, the coats hanging in front of me like a heavy curtain. I smelled leather and darkness.

And then the most amazing thing happened. The Mermaid appeared. I imagined her with my eyes closed and then she was inside the closet with me, holding my hands and my face. I reached out to hug her. I wrapped my arms around her waist. She knelt down. I unwrapped an arm so that I could pat her head. Her wavy hair felt as fluffy as a cloud. I took my hand and stroked her face. I traced her lips.

Then I leaned forward and kissed her. I ran my tongue along the closet walls and imagined it was in her mouth. I ran my arms up and down my body and pretended the Mermaid was loving me. We kissed each other for a long time. When I was finished and as full of love as I could get, I sank to the floor and put my knees under my chin. Coat sleeves hung in my face. I pretended they were the Mermaid's arms. They caressed me in a lovely way. I sighed into my hands and felt safe and warm. When I opened my eyes again, the Mermaid was gone.

But I would be okay. I knew how children and adults were supposed to love each other. And now I knew I could have that love any time I wanted, just by going into the closet, where everything was perfect.

Cara Marks

AURORA BOREALIS

1. You pour me another drink

I love the sound of liquid falling – a river splashing on stone, that pitter-patter of rain on the skylight, the mellifluous comfort of more wine in my cup. To let go of something impossible to hold on your own, with bare hands. To fill yourself up.

We sit on a wooden swing in the garden with swirly blue and yellow mugs that remind me of Greece, though I've never been. They're filled with Okanagan Pink Pinot Gris and freshly picked mint and raspberries. You're tipsy and want me to join you. You're sad. You're a mature man of new masculinity, think you're tougher if you show your feelings. But still you don't want to cry in front of me, your youngest child and only daughter. The boys have already gone home.

"The garden is beautiful," I say, because it is. It is barely edible – filled with Mama's flowers: clematis, chrysanthemums, zinnias, dahlias, a million ferns. Plum, pear, apple trees with fruit not yet ripe. A corkscrew willow by a dory-size pond. No lawn or lawnmower.

You wear a bathrobe without shirt or trousers. Socked feet slipped into flip-flops, legs crossed, your hair a thinning white side-parted mop. You wear Mama's glasses because yours are broken. The lenses are smudged. In your lap, you hold a pink carnation and your cup. Are we going to get drunk? There are two jugs full of wine and a bucket of berries. You sip and sip, roll a raspberry on your tongue.

The swing sits three and lazily sways, and I wonder how to approach the space between us. You are too far away to lean into, and I don't know how to give you comfort, if that is what you need. The sunlight staggers out of blushing clouds. The pond's edges stitched with apple blossoms, its musty smell intertwined with the flowers' sweetness.

I check my watch and say, "Soon we'll have cake."

Odd, to be surrounded by lush foliage not yet decaying, all these things we didn't plant.

2. Mama sings a Spanish ballad

A month ago, a week before she died, Mama stood in the garage with a paintbrush and an enormous canvas where a car could be. She was sixty-three and I was about to be thirty. Her hair all grey curls tucked under a teal scarf, tied above her forehead. She wore a denim smock over bare legs, naked feet splattered with paint. I sat on the floor, tip-toeing onto the canvas when I stretched out my legs. She painted Frida Kahlo flowers and snow-capped mountains and the northern lights. Her song delicate, her voice a coloratura contralto and I didn't understand the words, only *bella bella bella*, which she sang over and over and twirled, pink paint from her brush Pollocking the canvas and the walls.

"Do you like it?" she said, and stood in a dizzy sway. "It's not done yet."

She dropped into child's pose and leaned into the canvas, her knees and forearms freshly painted. She had always painted but wanted to be a poet. In cursive at the bottom corner of the canvas she wrote in baby blue with a skinny brush:

> *my bella—*
> *sweetness*
> *you are an O'Keeffe landscape,*
> *Rothko in the summer,*
> *Matisse in the morning*

> *you are the great and wild*
> *unknown known and*
> *I love you*

But how to say it, she would say, how to write love into poetry without using the word. Love, the word, weighs down a poem, she'd been told. How to tell me she loved me. And yet I always knew.

"You can have it for your birthday," she said.

"Where will I put it?"

She stretched out her arms, a crucifix covered in pink.

"Has he called?" I asked.

She crooked her head, tugged off the teal. She rose again with her feet at her insignia. "You can use it as a rug."

3. I pour you another as well and you yodel and we remember

We are drunk now. You are doing that thing with your hands where you twist the tip of each finger as if a cork you wish to unscrew, where really you just want a cigarette but you haven't smoked since 1983.

The sky bleeds off its colour and the swing rocks swifter now. You have removed your glasses and I wonder, can you still see me?

You guzzle the new wine in your mug and totter to the pond's edge.

I leave you there, for a moment, and meander to the kitchen to find the cake. I'm distracted by flowers along the way. I pick an enormous pale pink dahlia. The flower's twirled petals are soft and it's the size of my face. You've left your suitcase on the dining-room table and a pile of your clothes on the floor. I ease open the oven and am engulfed in its warmth and the smell of ginger and cinnamon. The cake has burnt because we are drunk and when I return to the garden you have jumped into the pond. You're up to your waist in milky green water and you splash and splash.

"*Yodelayheehoo*," you sing. "*Yodelayheehooooooooooooooo.*"

I tell you to get out, you'll drown, but I know you will not drown because the water is at your waist and I say you'll get hypothermia but it is September and it is a hot September and you are warm with wine and death is not your concern, not yours.

You say, "You have never loved."

"The cake is burnt," I say, and again you say *you have never loved.*

"*Yodelayheeeehooohoohoooooo-ooo-ooo-oo.*"

The cake is burnt but I hold it, I carry it on grandma's bright orange plate with a bowl of whisky-spiced whipped cream, to cover the burn. It's Mama's recipe, and your favourite at Christmas, and the only thing I can bake and yet I can't, couldn't quite. It is ginger cake and there was not enough ginger. I cracked one too many eggs and I did not wait for the butter to rest at room temperature. And yet I baked it.

I stand, unsteady, amidst zinnias. Their gold and red blossoms at my knees. I place the cake and the cream in the middle of the swing with two forks.

"The cake is burnt but there is cake," I say, "and I loved her."

"But why loved," you say. "Why *love-duh.*"

"Dad, you're going to catch a cold."

"It was so easy for you."

"Please, would you get out of there? You are so wet."

"It's raining," you say, and it has just begun to.

4. *Can you hear the Northern Lights?*

In August, Mama visited me in Squamish and we drove her pickup truck to Whitehorse to see you, to see if you would come home. We drove for two days straight because she could not wait.

She wanted to see the sun, how many hours it would stay in the sky, and when it fell she hoped for Aurora Borealis. She said it was bioluminescence in the sky, but I'd always thought bioluminescence looked like stars. She told me this at 3 a.m. parked on the side of the road an hour past Kitwanga, when we were both too tired to drive. I staggered almost into a dream, and when I woke the engine rumbled and it was barely 5 a.m., Mama in her fuchsia coat with her hood on, humming quietly.

We arrived at Uncle F.'s and found you on the front porch. The cabin surrounded by pines, its foundation tipping toward the slow river. You played guitar, barefoot in a black suit and a bomber hat.

Mama tripped out of the truck to kiss you but you said, "What are you doing here?"

Mama said she loved you and you repeated the question, *why are you here*.

Uncle F. swung open the screen door and gave Mama and me kisses on the cheek. He smacked your head like he'd have done when you were kids, and told you to get up.

You went there to hunt, to stay with Uncle F. and eat fresh moose, fresh fish. You killed a bison and packed its meat – we no longer called it a body – in brown paper in the freezer. Mama said, "What will you do with all this meat?" She'd been a vegetarian for forty years.

That night we listened to Bruce Springsteen and you and Uncle F. shotgunned cheap beer. Mama and I drank honeyed tea. Uncle F. smoked a cigarillo and called himself sophisticated. Mama held Jackal, the grey tabby cat, in her lap. We sat there, on the porch, waiting to see the light show – emerald, mauve, red ribbons shimmering by the stars. We wondered if it would come, if it would be enough. Mama fell asleep and you carried her to the sofa in the early morning. Uncle F. fell asleep, too, but we left him there. We lay with our backs on the oak floor of the porch, Jackal on your belly, rising and falling with your breath.

You said, "I'm not ready," and I let it linger.

I tried to find constellations, decipher abstract patterns and find their ancient myths and truths. Orion, Ursa Major, but that's all I found. Hazy green shone in the sky like headlights in fog and I asked was this it, should I wake up Mama? You said these were barely them, it wasn't worth it to wake her up.

I fell asleep there too and woke to you and Mama whispering in the kitchen, Mama's hushed tears, a caw of a crow, and the quiet rush of the river. You held each other, her face tucked into the lapels of your suit.

On the way home we stopped in Stewart again and Mama asked me to wait for a minute. She wanted to hike to the glacier, to touch it. It looked so close but took her hours to get there and back. The glacier stretched out between mountains and looked like the sky. I sat in the truck and waited. She shrunk, became a little pink bird flying away and away to touch the clouds.

"I'm sorry," she said, and I said it was fine, we have days to get home, and she said sorry for being hard to love. She said, "I think your dad finds me too hard to love."

I wondered what you'd say, why you stayed in Whitehorse, and what you both meant by love.

Edward Brown

REMEMBER ME

Ten minutes after the drop, George Bennett, alias George Dickson, was pronounced dead and his body cut down. Prone on the gravel in the exercise yard, Bennett's body – ankles and wrists pinioned – was heaved onto a flimsy cart and wheeled inside the facility. A black flag was hoisted up the gaol flagpole. The hangman, an ex-whiskey detective named English, removed the canvas mask required to conceal his identity, scratched at his coarse cheeks. Sometimes English went by the name Ellis.

Officials dispersed. Inmates dismantled the scaffold. A chatter of newspapermen departed. Outside the prison the festive throng of spectators thinned. A small crowd lingered by the Don Bridge, shaded by a copse of black locust trees.

English drew a small hardback book from inside his jacket and made notations with a dull pencil. Gathering the half-inch soaped rope into a butterfly coil, he untied the noose and placed the rope into a sack. He stood a moment and gazed into the gauzy white face of the rising sun. At the base of the wall behind him, the inmate assigned to dig Bennett's grave went at the earth with pick and shovel, quietly humming the chorus to "It Is Well with My Soul."

Before retiring to an unadorned apartment inside the gaol where he had slept the previous night, the hangman collected his forty-dollar fee from Governor Green. Undressing, he leaned over a washbasin, splashed warm water on his face. He lathered shaving soap in a mug and shaved his cheeks smooth. He gulped from a flask and changed into a new black suit. Sitting down heavily on the stained mattress, English unfolded a penny knife and cut lengths of rope from the cord that had recently launched Bennett into eternity. He placed personal effects into a carpet-bag patterned with rosebuds, then lay back on the cot and cat-napped.

An inquest was held pro forma in the small, black-and-white tiled prison hospital, austere as an anchorite's cell. Thirteen jurors were selected. Bennett's corpse was displayed on a table. The black sack covering the condemned's head was removed. The cord used to pinion his wrists and ankles was cut and the corpse stripped of clothing.

At five feet, two inches, Bennett was below medium height and weighed 126 pounds. He wore a black Van Dyke beard. Between purplish lips his tongue protruded, a black wedge of meat. His eyes were closed. His nose appeared to have been recently broken. Livid contusions marked his neck. His hands were a shade of blue similar to a morpho butterfly. The autopsy revealed congestion in the brain, lungs and heart. The posterior ligaments of his upper vertebrae were separated. As a result of the drop, his spinal column had dislocated.

Medical examiner's conclusion: Death was instantaneous.

The jury's verdict, unanimous: The condemned had experienced no pain.

~

It was forenoon when English approached the crowd lingering by the locust trees, rope sack and carpetbag slung over his shoulder. In his free hand he held up samples of rope, repeating, "Souvenir? Souvenir. Justice is done. The righteous rejoice. The honorable George Brown's killer, finished by *this* rope. An historic day. A souvenir?"

Horse blankets spread on the ground, a rank stench fouled the air as families fried carp livers, potatoes, and bay mussels on naphtha stoves, breakfasting in the fashion of a picnic. A knot of ragged men hovered around the mossy stump of an enormous oak tree, wagering on card games of Faro and jawing profanely at one another as they might in Sluttery's Tavern, a King Street groggery popular among this class.

A couple sat on the ground leaning against the spokes of a wagon wheel eating sliced June apples and paste made from cashews spread on three-day-old bread dipped into mugs of cold coffee. Playing in the box of the wagon, the couple's children, a girl with a pinched face in a shabby gingham dress and her younger brother took turns tormenting a wounded jaybird with a blunt stick. Harnessed at the front of the wagon, a gelded mule twitched his ears and whimpered. Eyes clouded the colour of zinc, the mule swayed his head, braying.

Piercing the jaybird through the wing, the girl chastised the mule, "Shut up, Guff. Or else you'll get it, too."

The crowd surrounded English. Boys climbed out of trees. Men in blue and white check vests and felt derbies ambled toward the hangman, rubbing their huge bellies and inhaling deeply from hooked ceramic smoking pipes. On the riverbank, a shoeless lunatic in overalls the locals called Vegetable hooted wildly as a silvery brook trout tugged at the end of his line. Vegetable's name was really Matthias. In summertime, Vegetable holed up under the Don Bridge. In winter, he secreted away to a nest he'd slung between webbed trusses in the attic of the smallpox hospital north of the gaol.

An emaciated teenage boy with a harelip and rags for clothing dangled from a limb, kicking his spindly legs. In a voice like bone pressed to an emery wheel, he recited a Bible verse about the powers of darkness, shouting at English, "What's it *feel* like, killing for a living?"

English's expression remained flat. Indecipherable. A weathered tombstone. By habit, or no, instinct, he sized up the changeling-like boy, calculating where the lad fit on the Table of Drops scale.

"Tell me your name, boy," he shouted.

A voice in the crowd cried, "What he's called doesn't matter—"

A second voice added, "He's Vegetable's."

Perched above the crowd, the slender boy repeated, "What's it *feel* like, killing for a living?"

Gazing into the boy's resinous eyes, English ignored the query, instead removing the hardback book from his jacket. Thumbing the onionskin pages, he calculated figures in his head and then jeered, "I approximate your weight at what, ninety pounds?" Guffawing, he studied the page in mock disbelief. "Would you believe to end a waif like you necessitates a twelve-foot drop?" English snickered, "Sorry boy, at that height likely I take your head off."

The boy heckled English. "I wear the armor. I'm not afraid of you or your rope. Still haven't answered, what's it *feel* like, killing—?"

"Well," English interrupted, "if you must know, it feels like, like a full stomach and a clean suit of clothing. It feels like the taste of costly bourbon." His nostrils flared. "It feels like a close shave and like the scent of a perfumed lady." Locking eyes with the crowd, he concluded, "It feels like a downy pillow at close of day." Tucking the book into his breast pocket, he clasped his hands and mocked, "At least from my end of the rope, anyway."

The hushed crowd erupted in laughter. The raw-boned boy appeared to shrink sizes.

"Now," English taunted, "Tell me, what's the feel of hunger? How does it *feel* to have the face of a praying mantis? Tell me, what's it feel like to be *insignificant*?"

The woman seated with her back to the wagon wheel leaped to her feet and beckoned English over. She snatched a sample of rope from the hangman. Strands of auburn hair came loose from her chignon. Her cheeks flushed as she clenched the fibrous twine, shoving the rope toward her husband. Face set in a moue, she sulked, "This is foul. I want it."

Obeying, her man paid English with money from his purse.

Pressing the rough cord to her breast, she turned a mock pirouette, perspiration glistening on her nape. With a hint of leer, she asked English, "How much of your rope to do me?"

~~~

After the hanging, Governor Green took breakfast. He instructed the chief turnkey to assign two inmates to prepare Bennett for burial, dressing the cadaver in clothing delivered the previous afternoon by Bennett's three siblings, Patience, William, and Julie, as well as a flaxen-haired gentleman in a waistcoat, striped trousers, and Christy stiff hat also named William. This second William went by Billy.

Upon arrival at the gaol gate, the foursome's way had been blocked by Vegetable, splayed on the ground. He rose to meet them and bowed himself with his face to the earth. Clasping the hems of Patience and Julie's matching blue satin polonaises, he wept, "Angels, turn aside. This household is unclean."

Julie knelt and, without malice, inquired, "What is your name?"

"I am the replacement, Matthias."

Julie retrieved a small, embroidered sachet containing a jot of lavender from her reticule and placed it in Matthias's filthy palm. Stepping around the senseless man, the others followed as she opened the gate and entered the prison grounds. From numerous cell windows, licentious inmates hooted obscenities.

They clawed at the air like confined passengers on a doomed ship.

Bald-faced hornets swarmed the mucronate opening of a papery, grey nest constructed in the architrave molding above the entrance door. Patience, tall, comely, and darkly complected, tugged the bell pull. In his whitewashed hands, William, a painter by trade, gripped a parcel of clothing wrapped in red butcher paper to his chest. Julie, the baby of the family, shaded herself under a parasol. Fearful of a wasp's sting, she pulled her grey straw hat trimmed with brown satin over her ears.

Carved into the alabaster keystone above the portico, the terrified likeness of Cronos, the father of time, gazed into a blank future. Following at least a dozen pulls, a turnkey with a tragic expression opened the heavy door.

"What?"

Patience murmured, "We're here to visit our brother."

Staring at them like they were zoo animals, he asked, "And?"

"And?" Patience cast a quick glance over her shoulder, "Allow us entry, please."

The turnkey studied Patience with agitation, suspicion. The intense midafternoon sunlight made everything appear increasingly queer.

"Who's your brother, then?"

"George Dickson," Patience said, before correcting herself. "Bennett, George *Bennett*."

"Bennett or Dickson? Which?"

"Bennett."

Their father was a coloured man of West Indian origin and unlike his brother and two sisters, Bennett had exhibited no Negroid features.

The turnkey was indignant. "Bennett? The white man?"

Patience unfolded the pass Sheriff Jarvis had provided granting permission to visit their brother in the death cell. The turnkey scrutinized the paper as sounds of carpentry, hammering, sawing, came from the rear of the gaol. Swatting at a wasp, Julie lost her balance, nearly toppling down the limestone steps. William reached for his little sister's elbow. He dropped the parcel. The contents spilled out.

The turnkey looked past Patience to Billy, "Can you vouch for the Negress?"

Billy's Adam's apple rose and fell before he said, "The Negress is my wife."

The door creaked closed. While they waited, a wasp stung Julie on the cheek. The white-hot sting brought her to tears. With help from Patience, she sat down on the steps, one hand pressed to her cheek.

Minutes lapsed before the turnkey reappeared. In a mordacious tone he snarled, "No."

"No? No, what?" Patience inquired.

"No visit," he smirked, "Not today."

"When? Tomorrow our brother—"

Julie pawed at her neckline, "My throat. I can't—"

William removed Julie's gold collar pin – engraved with her initials – from the collar of her shirtwaist and dropped it on the step. Billy rubbed the back of her hand and attempted to settle her, repeating, "Shh, shh. It's okay. It's okay."

"I don't understand," Patience pleaded, holding up Sheriff Jarvis's pass, "We're permitted."

Julie panted, gasped, "Breathing. Difficult."

The turnkey uttered, "He wants visits from none of you. Bennett's words, not mine."

The heavy door closed tight as a fist. Jowls swollen, Julie clawed her throat, wheezing, "I can't breathe—"

Face at the mull post, Patience pleaded, "Please. Please. At the very least, help my baby sister. She's only fourteen."

The door remained closed.

William gathered the contents of the parcel into a neat pile, and left the reassembled package on the steps. Taking to their legs, they crossed the Don Bridge to the public road. Prison labourers digging a ditch beside Gerrard Street paused to watch the foursome board an omnibus bound for the city.

~~~

After consulting a walking boss, turnkey Wilson, a jittery man with a pronounced overbite, pulled aside two inmates, Deacon and Mann, before their work gang set out to complete work at Riverdale Park.

Scheduled by the mayor to open in less than two weeks, swathes of the new park still required attention. Gangs of inmates had been at work laying walkways, constructing a rockery and fountain, planting double rows of saplings along the boulevard beside Sumach Street. They levelled the earth, cleared tracts of bosky, and backfilled a ravine. The rush was on to drain mosquito-infested, swampy lowlands near the sluggish, brown Don River. The work was grueling; the miasma emitted from the swamp, combined with the rancid stench wafting from Lamb's Blacking & Glue Manufactory immediately south of the parkland, was intolerable.

Wilson guided Deacon and Mann to the room containing Bennett's corpse. Deacon, a nasally woebegone grumbler as crooked as a corkscrew, was awaiting trial for housebreaking and petty larceny. Once set upon with a cricket bat, portions of his skull bone appeared to float under the flesh of his shaved head. Where his right eye had been knocked out during the assault, dense scar tissue formed a sphincter-like opening on his face.

Fourteen-year-old Mann, eyes as blue as deep water, had been sent up fifteen days for drunkenness. Two days remained on his sentence. Despite recent setbacks, for the most part, Mann was a happy-go-lucky fellow.

In infancy, he had been left partially deaf after a bout of typhoid he was not expected to survive. Gamins he ran with called their cheery friend "Mann Lucky," "Just Lucky" or "Lucky." Mann pledged to himself that upon release he would leave the gaol, find a situation, and be done with the city. Ages ago he lost his pop and his ma and his siblings to smallpox. He had no one.

Resembling a grotesque Jumeau doll, George Bennett's sutured and stitched body lay unclothed on a table. A splendid black coffin ferried from Cobourg – the town of his birth – on the night steamer, *Mirth*, and delivered before dawn by a teamster from Small's Wharf, stood propped in the corner. The lid displayed St. Peter's inverted trefoil cross. Items of clothing sat neatly folded on a sturdy workbench.

Wilson turned up the gas, washing the room in sickly, yellow light. The prisoners paused at the sight of Bennett. Slowly, Mann removed his cap, crossed himself.

Deacon chortled, "What's this, then?"

Turnkey Wilson shoved the inmates forward. "Clothe it and get it coffined."

"Wait now," Deacon whined. "This is women's work. Strumpets in the west wing could know better what to do with this bloke." Glancing in the corner, Deacon sized up the coffin, and added, "A papist, too."

"Governor's orders," Wilson barked. "Get on with it before he's hardened."

Deacon and Mann set to dress Bennett in fineries of the day: a double-breasted pine green, sable brushed, frock coat with matching vest and trousers. Size five stacked heel cordovan leather shoes. A white collar.

Loosely tying a barrel knot around his own neck before passing the tied cravat to Deacon, Mann gently cupped the back of

Bennett's head, raised it slightly allowing Deacon to slip the black satin cravat over the scalp and around the dead man's neck. Wilson watched idly from the doorway.

Mann wiped a spot of grime from Bennett's ashen cheek with his frayed cuff, grooming the dead man's thick moustache with his fingertips. Mann asked, reverently, "Who is he?"

Straightening the cravat, Deacon shrugged. Mann instructed, "Not too tight."

Wilson leaned in the doorway, chewing his thumbnail as the pair retrieved the coffin. Mann grasped Bennett's shoulders, Deacon his ankles, and together they lowered the body into the box.

Mann knelt, smoothed Bennett's lapels, patted the dead man's firm chest. Lid set in place, the white metal thumbscrews remained unfastened.

In a pasture behind the gaol a dog barked.

Deacon and Mann turned to Wilson. Mann asked, deferentially, "Sir? Now?"

Cast in yellow gaslight, the men appeared jaundiced. Wilson instructed each to turn out the pockets of their Garibaldi jackets. Without hesitation, Mann complied. Deacon stared at his boots, "I didn't nick nothin'."

Wilson jabbed his billy into Deacon's throat. "Like I said, turn 'em."

Deacon removed an engraved silver timepiece, a Dickson family heirloom with cylinder movements, and a lady's gold collar pin from his pocket.

Wilson seized both.

"A fine timepiece," Deacon stammered nervously. "Too fine to bury."

The turnkey held up the timepiece, studied it. "Valuable," he murmured, and before slipping the watch into his pocket glanced at the open doorway. "Valuable, indeed."

Deacon and Mann fastened the coffin lid in place. Wilson watched, hovering over their shoulders. Turning the collar pin over in his hand, he asked, "Either of you knew of this man?"

"Knew 'em? No, only that he ended another man."

Mann asked, "Which man?"

Wilson winked, "*The* man. Brown." He tossed the collar pin at Mann, who reflectively snatched it out of the air. The turnkey murmured, "Son, in this life, there's profit in not knowing."

"Pardon?"

"There's profit. In not knowing," Wilson repeated himself, louder.

Mann sighed. "Oh. Profit. Of course."

Mann tightened the final screw on Bennett's coffin and squeezed the collar pin in his palm. The coffin was placed on a cart. Wilson ordered, "To yard."

Mann pushed from the rear. The exercise yard was ablaze with sunlight. Mann leaned down, placed his boyish face close to the seam where lid and coffin joined and breathed, "Remember me."

With these final words seeping into the dead man's box, Bennett joined the choir invisible in the ground. Rev. Father Egan recited a benediction. Puffs of incense from the polished brass censer drifted above the exercise yard, over the wall, over the river, over trees, over public roads, over Riverdale Park, to the top of the sky.

≈

Upon his liberty, Mann was true to his word. He found a situation to convey him away from the city, replying to an ad in *The Globe* seeking agents to sell chromolithograph portraits of the late Hon. George Brown in townships throughout the province. He earned thirty-three cents on the dollar, plus a stipend for lodging.

With the take from a poker match he purchased eel-skin trousers, a pair of Chelsea boots, and a green vest. He sat in a hair-cutter's chair for his first fifteen-cent haircut.

The collar pin given to him by turnkey Wilson pinned to his vest, he walked the highway between Toronto and Cornwall, hawking the likeness of George Brown on a plate.

"Souvenir? Souvenir. An historic day. A souvenir."

Passing through Cobourg on the road from Kingston, he encountered a downcast young Black woman in a satin polonaise, sitting on a covered porch, alone on a comfortable swing chair.

"Hello," he greeted her. "I am thirsty."

She offered water.

The most exquisite lady he'd ever encountered eyed the collar pin fixed to his chest.

For perhaps the first time in a long time, she smiled. "The pin. Where did you come by it?"

"A long story."

"Sit. Please. Join me so I might hear."

William John Wither

THE BULBOUS IT WITH NO EYELIDS

The world became obtuse and she knew it was time to get up.

The glue on her alarm clock held as she turned it off; its spirit level pooled to one side as it passed the point of silence. As she leaned up, she leaned back so as to not fall into the distant corner of the room. The waxing angle left almost nothing shifted. Everything had been bolted in its proper place. Even the glass she took to bed was still nestled into the deep plastic well affixed to the bed's side; a sippy cup top containing the viscous content from splattering into the seams of the floor.

She placed her foot into the worn widgets welded into the ground and stood. Her lower back balanced her as she descended into the crater of her apartment, an ostrich in imaginary arches.

She opened her dresser to find a matted wad of clothes fallen from their hangers. She dug through the cold lump for a knit sweater that would cozy her climb to the stage. The less it stared, the colder it got, its attention drawn elsewhere for a time. Hopefully, only for a time.

In the fridge, three eggs had broken from the agitated slump, but were fresh enough to be scraped up and settled into a pan. Some

fixtures were too variable to withstand the angle. Only the afflu-
ent could perch all their propers with custom molds. Molds for
eggs and egg timers and egg holders and the spoons to crack them
with. She was not of them, though she often dreamt of how their
faces would disintegrate to cinder and pulp if she were to hit
snooze. Just once.

She thought of this again as she threaded the laces through her
inverted stilettoed boots, those perched on foot-high oak blocks
and grooved rubber that could grip stone, and placed them into
the rivets. No longer could she turn. Could only face north. Only
towards her destination. Only until the world straightened itself.

She descended backwards to the frame of her door, pawing
behind for the knob before entering the hall. This was only a
minor inconvenience when compared to having one's room on
the south-leaning side. To have innumerable clutter wank under
your door or having to exert yourself as you crawled up the slanting mound toward the rest of your apartment. And if you were to
fall, which many did, breaking a bone would be welcomed over
the threat of impalement, blinding, or death. The old and feeble
died this way, desperately reaching for a carton of orange juice or
the bathroom door. Many were found lying in the corner in the
congeal of their own excrement, too spent to stand or cry for help.

No, it was better to be on the north side. She had earned that
much. Deserved more.

As she closed the door, another girl came shuffling down the hall
toward her. No words were exchanged, only a look of mutual
acknowledgement. There wasn't much to say, nor comfort to
instill. It was the protocol of a punch card, a line to wait in, a shift
to fill, a time between then and later.

They began their Siamese scuttle through the vacant hall. Summer crabs on beechwood. Quiet tacks. Together they passed a door with the sounds of guttural hacking behind, the putrid stream of vomit slurping through the bottom crack of the door and collecting into a grooved drainage pipe beneath; a modern amenity many weren't afforded. Buildings too old or poor had the waste slip across into the southern room, a trail left to slip on. Car keys, used condoms, off-cast in any form could follow in the lean. Yes, the north was preferred.

They walked down three flights of stairs to the ground level, the elevator, useless, meant only for movement along a vertical plane. A large woman on the eighth had tried once, but the friction fissured a hot box of screaming sinew that incinerated her before it reached the bottom. Their building smelled of roasted skin for a week. They told the children it was tuna. They all pitched in to buy some.

In the deep gash of early morning light, other women already walked in near silence. A mixture of sleep deprivation and mental acuity. To think of what only *it* liked, the disgust of having to think it.

In the distance, the crest of *it*s head plummeted a thick, cool shade on the pebbled road-turned-temporary hill. Hundreds of women clopped the rugged, slanting terrain; felt like the horses they ate. Around them, the stacking shutters of the laneway remained closed, quiet, restricted from the pilgrimage, asleep, feigning sleep.

A woman stopped to allow them into the herd, her calves a deep purple. Shins covered in crackled skin.

"I've come from the forty-fifth," she said.

"That's a long way to climb," said the other.

"Can you make it the remaining twelve?" asked the woman.

"What choice do I have."

What choice did they have? Participation was no longer voluntary. *Its* appetite had grown. Long ago, longer than can be remembered, it was an act of pageantry. Girls in their most evocative wares paraded for the honour of *it*'s attention. Tapestries of lapis and crushed shells. Of candy wrappers contorted into weave baskets for breastplates. To earn *it*'s gaze cast admiration and accommodation and tuna and fine wines and fine things. Real butter. Butter to butter all provisions. Cows with udders of silk and envy.

To one, *it* would look, and the axis would slowly, creakingly lurch as the scabbing silhouettes of *it*'s eyes focused on *her*.

Then, one day, *her* became *them*. Pageantry dissolved as park fair candyfloss as two became four became more became countless bodies stacked like needle sticks hoping to make fire. Age ranges sipping from the fringes of innocence and old. *It* wanted what *it* wanted without shame or consequence, felt nothing toward them beyond *it*'s biology.

But always women. Only women. Always throughout history, they danced. Treated as though they were no more than the parts that comprised them.

They had tried men, then combinations of men, though only once they knew of *it*'s insatiableness, the bleeding of *it*'s desires. But no interest was shown, the coldness remaining, the world continued in its tilt. So they sat at home – the fathers and the brothers and the male relatives one could muster to look after their own – gently stroking calm into the curls of sleeping children, themselves sick with the helplessness of circumstance.

And so, the women climbed. The women and the girls and the mothers and the daughters, to the peak to perform. Step by oblique step.

The eleventh, then the tenth. The chaffing ankles and knees and murmurs of discomfort. The clicking of cobbled stone in the dense cold. And then the screams. The women braced themselves against their neighbours as bodies came hurtling down the slanting tarmac.

A large, elderly broad with blistering skin falling from the sixth. A limp addict careening from the third. Legs given out from the climb. They fell, flailing, screaming until a rough blow to the head left them lame. Dozens would die this way, the climb too far for those in the lower boroughs. This is how *they* weed out the weak, the broken, the unbeautiful, the poor of character of mind. So, the streets were quiet, except for the screaming.

By the fifth, the woman to her right looked beyond reprieve, a sack of regurgitated turkey meat.

"Just a few more blocks," the other one said. The older woman said nothing. All was concentration. One foot beyond the next.

Then another scream.

An arm to brace, but the old woman kept climbing. "One more step. One more step. One more step." The body hit her deep in her gut. She pulsed back with a ripping pop, her body attaching to the fallen as she, too, fell from the fourth. But not all of her. One more step had left her left leg, from knee to heel, in the street's socket. Another woman calmly removed it and supplanted her own in its place.

There was no time to mourn. No time to think of the woman, of who she left behind. None of it could matter now. All emotions and things subject to *it*.

The arches ahead framed a dark, fleckless courtyard. Nothing grew there. There was no light for anything to grow there. The bulbous stubble of the eclipsing *it* made it a land of muddy, crusted swamp, of macerated clumps of eroded earth that cracked under their collective weight. The sound of crème brûlée crust as they paced through the yard to the wooden pier that separated them from the sand at the edge of the world.

Lopsided lockers sat tinged with salt and rust as the women placed their angled platoons of boots into the provided receptacles. Their boots were always carefully sorted so they could be reclaimed, but all other clothing was thrown into a large slosh of sleeved garment in the pier's centre. No one wanted the physical reminders of the dance, no association could supersede it, so they made a pile, one which they'd pilfer afterwards for something new to walk home in.

The lockers shut, the lapping sand that swallowed the pier filled the crevasses of their toes. It poured onto the wood like an hourglass on its hind legs, letting balance back into their heels. They walked towards the shore, huddled, scant.

The women looked to the granules of sand, to the pooling sea, to *it*. There *it* stood, or so they thought *it* stood. To peek over the ledge on either side or at the sea's end yielded no definite answer.

*It*s foam white skin descended into a dense fog of nothingness to an indeterminable depth. Only *it*s expanding waist of reflective flesh formed from the nether cloud and scaled with a bark of dark hair to *it*s neck, the neck they saw at this very moment, as *it*s head looked away from them.

It looked like a man, like the ones found singing on a riverbank or picking flowers from a garden or holding doors how you do, but infinite times larger and of only the motor skills necessary to rotate *it*s head and stare. Stare through eroded gashes of unformed lids, ones that seemed to have been scissored away like loose fabric. They could not see those eyes now, the ones that stared at the other land on the other side.

As the women leaned back, they could see the other side floating a hundred miles away, on *it*s other shoulder. It was tilted too, but of their inverse in every way. *Their* sea sunk off into the ether below. Their beach glistened in summer sun and was void of any discernible being. They had heard the alarm too; had locked themselves inside to pray. Please do not eat our children. Please do not swallow us whole. Like a plate leaned to lick, the other side tilted towards *it*s face, *it*s opening mouth, as *it* aimed to engulf them. Only a matter of time if the women did nothing.

They had never spoken a word to the other side, so to help each other had become an unspoken agreement. They could not, if they wanted to. Nothing traversed the void within which the bald, naked, white "man" stood. Never their words or screams. Coloured flags said as much as they needed to, but had long been worn out. They had lost their purpose. No one side was better off than the other. No advancements surpassed another. Nothing was happening over here that wasn't happening over there to them.

And never was the angle between the two suspended clumps of land so acute that one could fly down to the other, even if they wanted to, especially with the thought of a loose gust careening you into *it*s shoulder blade or saggy load. To be stranded on *it* with no hope of rescue. To know what *it* felt like, hard pebbles or moist pudding.

So, it was an unspoken agreement. To perform the ritual. To draw *it*s attention, and so the women began.

A three-four waltz blared from the PA system, enough to make some of their ears bleed, some stuffed with cotton. The record had long since lost its appeal as a legitimate piece of music, was the droning of ripping nails and splitting tongues, but a favourite of *it*. Anything that helped.

Shoulders cuffed shoulders in rhythmic pulsation. The privacy screen had been draped from the pier, though no one had the taste to watch, to see their loved ones splayed out like puzzle pieces forming an image they never wanted to see.

All eyes stared up at *it* during the dance, the amorphousness of hands helping to conceal identity, to be a neighbour or the butcher's wife or daughter. To not know the ramifications of action. To become one.

And *it*s body lurched, and the ground they stood on with *it*. Women fell forward into the surf, their bodies weighed down with silt and smothered under churning feet. They helped who they could back up, but they must perform, lest they lose *it*s attention. Girls cried for their mothers when they knew they shouldn't, had been told their tears were not part of the ritual, that *it* liked flesh, not what leaked from it.

And as *it* turned, so did the axis, so did the weather. The shivering of knees was clapped with eyelashes of colour, pirouettes of warm spring dust. The women spread out, aiming to be felt in *its* peripherals. The shifting mass had soaked the ground with the rising sea, had made clay soup to stir with the early crest of the shore. The drowned now floated in it. They would be retrieved later if they hadn't drifted away.

Its face now became perpendicular. *Its* swollen eyes never peeked until *it* was ready; until *it* had interpreted all sounds and smells. *It* was a connoisseur of *its* delights.

A small hand grabbed the woman's. A hand that had had enough, that wanted to go home. The woman fought the urge to relinquish herself from its grasp, for it hindered the flows she pronounced. It had been her hand at a time, looking for her mother in the folds, then grabbing any hand, lost in a shopping centre. So, she held it.

The razored pocketfuls of *its* eyes peered onto them as *it* breathed in and exhaled warm air. With her eyes closed, it felt of a gentle breeze, its moisture salty from the wake. Arms had bruised, knees had buckled, tired sand people covered in the yellow warming light, dancing to a song they no longer heard.

The other land in the distance had become a vanilla wafer, its undercarriage of sediment barely above their own. Was it even worth saving? Was *this* even worth saving? The woman wondered. They danced for those they had never met, so they didn't skid into *its* salivating mouth. Maybe *they* thought the same thing. Maybe they were just waiting for *it not* to look. Just once. And the humiliation would be over.

But a hand still grabbed hers, so she performed, and *it* looked.

By the time *it* had locked its gaze in place, summer had come, *it*s jaw slowly opening, feathering their city ever so slightly higher, unnoticeable among any with enough energy left to care. They had stopped. A silence without congratulation or celebration. The hand in hers left as quickly as it came. She never looked. Only to the sea, to the floating carapaces of the trampled. She and a group of others began the process of pulling in the ones they could reach.

One was old, another small and porcelain, a cracked doll, and another was the girl from down the hall. All were dragged to shore and covered with beach towels of lilies and tundra swans, pulled into the provided tent.

She walked back to the locker while the rest of the women scoured over the pile of remaining clothes. The scraps left for those who had stayed to help. The woman took two sets of boots with her – hers and the others – and nothing else. Barefoot on the cobbled street, she heard the shutters rise, the children cry of joy for ice milk on a humid day. They were going to the beach, after all. She was going to rest, but only for a time.

Mark Paterson

MY UNCLE, MY BARBECUE CHICKEN DELIVERYMAN

The first time I met my uncle Sidney, he pulled a wad of money out of his pocket and laid five bills of different denominations side-by-side on a coffee table. There was a green one-dollar bill, a brownish-orange two, a blue five, a purple ten, and a red fifty. He told me I could pick one to keep.

I chose green.

I don't have any of my own, authentic memories of this event – I was barely two years old when it happened – but the pictures I see in my mind are as vivid as a movie. The story had that much of an impact on me. My mother told it to me when I was seven, while we were packing up our house on Chapleau Street, a few days before we moved to the Normandie Apartments. Cardboard boxes, scavenged from the garbage bin behind the grocery store, were stacked all over the place. My mother had put me to work on the lower levels of a shelving unit we had in the living room, packing books and knickknacks into a box that had once held pineapples.

Tucked in among the books, I found a photo album. It had a burgundy cover that felt like velvet, soft to the touch. I opened it, and flipped through pages filled with pictures of familiar places and faces: my grandparents' house in black and white, the big oak tree in the front yard alongside a second, slightly smaller one that I had only ever known as a stump, and my grandmother and grandfather themselves, younger and less wrinkled. I recognized my mother's face as a child and, in other photos, as a teenager, as well as those of my uncles Morris and Kevin. There were pictures taken in different rooms inside the house, out on the front lawn, and on the shore of the river that was just steps from the yard.

As I went through the photographs, I kept noticing the presence of another child; a third boy. I didn't recognize him, but my mother and my uncles posed with their arms wrapped around his shoulders, laughing beside him, leaning into him.

I called my mother over.

I remember her wearing a light blue bandana with a paisley pattern atop her head, the one she usually tied on when she tackled a big job around the house. A Band-Aid, blackened in spots by dirt, was wrapped around the tip of one of her thumbs. I pointed at one of the pictures in the album: a black and white, informal group shot taken on my grandparents' balcony. In the photo, my grandfather was lounging, cigarette in hand, on his chaise longue, surrounded by teenaged versions of my mother, Uncle Morris and Uncle Kevin, and the mystery boy. He was sporting a crewcut, and wore a striped T-shirt and dark, knee-length shorts. I tapped my finger right on the boy's chest. "Who's that?"

After learning of my uncle Sidney's existence and hearing the story of my first and only encounter with him, all I could think about was the fifty-dollar bill I had left on the table. For days, regret weighed down on me. I fantasized about what I could do with such a tremendous amount of money, as if – had I only chosen the red bill – the fifty dollars would have somehow still been at my disposal, unspent, five years later. The toy *Millennium*

Falcon in the Consumers Distributing catalogue was going for less than fifty dollars. There'd have been enough left over for action figures.

I formed a link in my mind between Sidney and money. I cast my newfound uncle in the role of the mysterious benefactor, the person who was going to appear again one day and rescue my mother and me. Sidney would buy me *Star Wars* toys. Sidney would pay for the new catalytic converter our car needed. Sidney would put us back in a real house.

When my thoughts wandered, I would wonder what kind of a person Sidney might be. Was he anything like my other uncles? Morris smoked a pipe, baked luscious vanilla cakes every now and then, and once took me out on his boat for a whole day of fishing. Kevin kept two baseball gloves in the trunk of his car and would invite me to play catch with him out on my grandparents' front lawn. I never even had to ask.

Morris and Kevin both possessed a dry sense of humour, always quick with a joke or a funny retort, and they liked to tease. Growing up, I studied my uncles' style of humour, tried to emulate it, and hoped to be, one day, as amusing as them. They poked fun at their wives, ganged up on my mother, and joined my grandfather at baiting my grandmother, confusing her with absurd questions: "Is it spring forward and fall back? Or is it spring back and fall forward?" Morris stood up from his seat on the balcony and, after making a big show of moving his chair out of the way, demonstrated with great seriousness how it was more natural to fall forward than backward. My grandmother's eyes narrowed with uncertainty. Puffing on her cigarette, she pondered the question out loud for a time (while Morris, Kevin, and my grandfather exchanged mischievous looks). Eventually, she settled on fall forward, only to be immediately talked into fall back by Kevin. Then my grandfather cut in and argued for my grandmother's original choice. They went around and around in this circle until my grandmother, exasperated, sprang from her chair and marched toward the front door. In a wretched tone, she made one last remark before disappearing into the house, an utterance that set the men to whooping: "I don't know what we have to go and change the clocks for anyway!"

There was one particular Sunday visit to my grandparents' house when the usual happy, jocular atmosphere was noticeably absent. This was right after my aunt Christine – Kevin's wife – underwent breast reduction surgery. Everyone spoke softly, and seemed to move about cautiously. The men cast their eyes downward, studying the flaking grey paint on the balcony's floorboards. The women went out of their way to make sure Christine was comfortable – my grandfather even joined in the effort, offering her his chaise longue – but no one even hinted as to why. Several moments of uncomfortable silence passed; the robins in the oak tree provided the only sounds.

Then Kevin diffused the mood.

"So," he quipped, raising both of his hands a little, flexing his fingers, "I guess you all heard I got a hand reduction."

Those Sunday visits to my grandparents' house were an indulgence. Heaping plates of spaghetti, pastries for dessert (and sometimes Morris's cake), cousins to play with in a big yard at the edge of the river, and even though the water was polluted by then the shoreline seemed to me vast: rich with flat skipping stones, croaking bullfrogs hiding in tall reeds, and, after rains, soggy mud that sucked your boots down with satisfying slurping sounds. The apartment my mother and I lived in was cramped. Our little television only got decent reception from three English channels. There was a narrow patch of grass out in front of the building, but it was flanked by a handmade sign on a stake that warned all to keep off it. Though she usually resisted, I asked my mother often about Sidney. I wanted to keep his memory fresh in her mind, to strengthen our tenuous connection to him and to his money.

How I wished she would just pick up the telephone and give her brother a call.

The riches that I believed my estranged uncle possessed were enough of a reason to bring his name up with regularity, but, in time, another presented itself to me. It was the way my mother reacted whenever I raised the subject. She would exhale audibly. Her forehead would crease and her eyes would squint. I relished the sound and sight of such anguish. Using my power to elicit this torture was a great and guilty pleasure.

Gradually, I squeezed some information out of her: Sidney was the third of my grandparents' four children, younger than my mother by two years; growing up, he had been a gifted hockey and football player, and once broke his arm playing the latter; shortly after getting his driver's licence, he accidentally backed over the neighbours' cat on his way out of the driveway, and he wept when he went next door to tell them; he was living somewhere in Montreal now; he had married young but was divorced, and his two children from that marriage, a girl and a boy – older cousins I'd never met – had years ago moved away with their mother to Arizona.

At long last, on a Saturday morning when I was ten, the doorbell interrupted *Jonny Quest*. My mother threw a robe over her holey pajamas and answered the door. Out on the step, unannounced and unexpected, was Sidney. My mother appeared happy to see her brother, but I saw the furrow on her brow.

My uncle's face was tan. His hair was dark and cropped short like in that old photograph. He was not dressed the way I imagined a man of wealth would be. He wore thick, beige work boots, dark blue work pants, and a matching work jacket that, on the breast, featured an alarm bell logo. He said he had just finished an installation job in the neighbourhood and, seeing as he didn't get up to Montclair very often, thought he'd drop by. He had been surprised when he stopped at our old house on Chapleau Street and discovered we no longer lived there. He found our current address in the telephone book at a pay phone, and got our apartment number from the landlord, who'd been mowing his precious lawn outside the complex.

Sidney looked at the couch in the living room, empty now that I had joined him and my mother in the entrance to our place. He glanced in the direction of the opening to our little kitchen. He turned to my mother. "Ralph sleeping?"

My mother's face contorted; she looked irritated and mystified at the same time. She put a hand on my shoulder. "It's going on five years now since Ralph left."

Sidney blinked. His face registered a measure of surprise, but he promptly erased this with a smile. He ruffled my hair with an air of familiarity. He called me Bobby, not Robert, like we were old pals, as if only a few days – and not eight years – had passed since he'd last seen me. He was taller than my mother by a head. They had the same laugh – booming but clipped – and the same small, blue eyes.

"Hey," Sidney said suddenly, his face aglow. He reached into the pocket of his jacket and fished about. I got very excited. I was convinced I was about to get a chance at redemption. Surely my uncle's hand would come out of the pocket holding a bundle of money, bills of different colours. This time I'd know exactly what I was doing.

But it was only a stack of alarm stickers, the kind you put in a window or on a door to warn off burglars. Sidney slipped the top sticker from the stack and presented it to me like it was a Christmas present. Then, with the rest, he turned to my mother. "Let's put a few of these up. Even if you don't have an alarm system, it still gives the idea."

My mother said, "We're renting."

Sidney ignored this statement and, without hesitating, proceeded to place a sticker on the little frosted window in our front door. He went around to the windows in every room of the apartment and did the same. My mother followed him as he did this, a pained, forced smile on her face.

Not ten minutes later, Sidney was gone again.

My mother fished an empty margarine tub out of the garbage can and filled it with hot water from the sink. She took a butter knife out of the utensil drawer. It took her the rest of the morning to remove all of those stickers.

Nearly another decade passed without a word or sign from Sidney. A decade that saw both of my grandparents die; my grandmother first, of a staph infection, speculated to have been contracted at some point after cutting herself on the edge of a can of baked beans she'd opened for my grandfather's lunch; within a year he was gone, too, discovered in his bed, tucked under the covers, appearing no less peaceful than he did when he was sleeping. Morris got into some trouble with government auditors and had to sell his beloved Hewes Bonefisher to pay off the back taxes he owed. And over Thanksgiving weekend in 1988, Kevin's bladder became blocked. He and Christine were separated by then, but it was she who went to pick him up and rushed him to the hospital, my uncle in agony, doubled over in the back seat of her car, unable to squeeze out a single drop. It took emergency surgery to remove the stones.

And while my interest in my absentee uncle Sidney never truly waned, my teen years brought new diversions and pursuits to contend for my attention. Girls, punk rock, parties, and strategies to buy beer at the dépanneur while underage demanded much of my time. But every once in a while, Sidney would still enter my thoughts. Though my encounter with him and his alarm stickers had punched some holes in my beliefs about his money, I still allowed the fantasy of rescue, of a surprise inheritance, and even of a replacement father to play out in my mind.

With precious few appearances over the course of so many years, I wondered if Sidney was a recluse, an eccentric, or a combination of the two. Whatever the truth might have been, my uncle was exotic. Knowing he was out there, somewhere, and that I was related to him, made me feel just a little bit remarkable.

I left Montclair when I was nineteen. My mother had been hinting at taking a cheaper but smaller place in the Normandie complex, planning to give up a room of her own for an old sofa bed Kevin was looking to get rid of. I was about to start university, and had already been toying with the idea of moving out. I wasn't going to stay under those circumstances, sleeping in the comfort of a bedroom while my mother spent her nights tossing and turning on a fold-out couch in the living room. I had a student loan and a part-time job at the hot dog and pizza counter at the Club Price in Laval. A new warehouse was opening in Montreal, in Pointe-Saint-Charles. They were looking for employees willing to transfer.

Moving out also meant gaining some needed distance from my mother. She'd always done her best for me, but in my later teen years a kind of sadness came over her. She took up smoking, or, as I later learned, took it up again after having quit for nearly twenty years. She cried in the bathroom a lot. She must have thought I couldn't hear her behind the closed door, beyond her constant flushing of the toilet.

I found a little apartment in Notre-Dame-de-Grâce. It took only a minute to walk from my place up to Sherbrooke Street, where I could catch the 24 bus for the ride downtown to McGill. If a bus didn't come right away, I'd just start walking. Sometimes I walked all the way to school, ignoring the buses that passed along the way. There was so much to see: restaurants, stores, churches, monuments. There were signs and posters pasted to walls and to the sides of mailboxes, announcing concerts, garage sales, lost cats, and free symposiums with titles like *Secrets of the*

Ancient Druids and *Unlocking Your ESP Potential.* I felt like I had joined a gripping, much larger world.

One thing that fascinated me on these walks was that I found myself surrounded by hundreds of people – people on foot, on bicycles, in cars and in buses – and yet I was all alone. In Montclair I couldn't make it two blocks down the main street of town before seeing someone I knew. Anonymity was a new feeling for me, and it was surprisingly enjoyable.

I fell into a routine of classes, shifts at the Club Price (where I'd moved up in the world to a position at the Membership counter), reading and studying (not enough), falling asleep after the midnight *Star Trek* rerun on CBC, and, most Thursday nights, going out drinking with a handful of friends from Montclair who had also moved downtown. Near the end of October, I met someone.

It happened in the basement laundry room of my apartment building, where the light was dim and the ceiling was exposed. The room consisted of two washing machines, two dryers, and a rickety wooden chair. She was sitting in the chair the first time I saw her. It was a Friday night; a vague ache still lingered in my head, residue of the pitchers of beer I'd shared the night before at the Cock 'n Bull. She was wearing plaid flannel pajama bottoms and a grey, baggy Concordia University sweatshirt. She was reading a paperback. She had dark hair, tied back in a ponytail, and a pretty face that made me feel shy.

She looked up from her book as I entered the room with my garbage bag full of dirty clothes. Our eyes met and we exchanged polite hellos. I found both washing machines in use.

"Mine's almost done," she offered.

"Oh," was all I could think to say.

"Like, two minutes, max," she added. "It's on spin now."

I placed my bag of laundry on the concrete floor and leaned against the wall. I looked at anything but the woman in the chair.

"Have you been living here long?" she asked me.

"A couple of months," I said. "Since September."

"You're a student?"

"I'm at McGill."

"In what?"

"History."

"What are you going to do with that?" she asked. I had fielded this question more than a few times since starting school, but her tone was sunnier than what I was used to, more curious than skeptical. "Are you going to become a history teacher?" She was genuinely enthusiastic.

"That's the plan," I replied, feeling a little gratified. I looked at the cover of her book, Leonard Cohen's *Beautiful Losers*. "And you? You're in English?"

"Commerce."

I glanced at her book again and, despite myself, raised my right eyebrow.

"Oh, this is just for fun." She waved the book a little and closed the cover on a finger, keeping her place. "It's my second time reading it, actually. I'm sort of crazy about Leonard Cohen."

"That's cool," I said, hoping I sounded at least a little cool myself.

One of the washing machines rattled to a noisy stop. My new acquaintance sprang from the chair. With one less machine at work, it was decidedly quieter in the room than it had been before. "I'm Cynthia, by the way," she said.

"Robert," I mumbled in reply. "Bobby. Rob."

A grin appeared on Cynthia's face. There was a measure of warmth and a measure of humour behind that smile. "Pleased to meet you Robert Bobby Rob."

Over the following weeks, I ran into Cynthia in the laundry room a few more times, and often in the apartment building stairwell.

Sometimes, we'd find each other on the same bus heading to or from downtown. Conversations materialized easily, mainly thanks to Cynthia's gentle and genuine inquisitiveness. Her questions made me feel special. It wasn't long before I was beginning each day with the hope that our paths would somehow cross.

By December, with finals upcoming, Cynthia and I were holding nightly marathon study sessions together at her place. We worked side-by-side at her long, simple white Ikea desk. Leonard Cohen watched over us; Cynthia had stuck the *Songs from a Room* album cover to the wall above the desk. I had found it, used, at Cheap Thrills and bought it for her not long after we had shared our first kiss. I should have guessed Cynthia already owned every Leonard Cohen recording, but she seemed touched by the gift. She said a second copy would make an awesome poster.

I never saw anyone work so hard. Unlike me, Cynthia didn't wander over to the window for a peek outside. She didn't lie on the floor and stare at the ceiling. The TV remained off. If I spoke to her, I would inevitably have to repeat myself – she only looked up from her notes when she was ready to. Soon I was inspired to put in a better effort, to try and match Cynthia's diligence, and I forced myself to bear down. She'd poke me with the eraser end of her pencil when I'd fall asleep in my books.

Two-litre bottles of Pepsi and fast-food deliveries sustained us. Pizza, mostly, but we ordered souvlaki one night, and poutines on another. One Friday, we decided to call for barbecue chicken.

We placed our order, pooled some money together, and got back to studying. After a while, Cynthia stood up from the desk to go to the bathroom. An idea, a little prank, had been on my mind that night. I saw my chance to put it into action.

Cynthia had this nightgown that she never wore; garishly old fashioned, ankle-length, purple, and decorated with white frills at the shoulders and around an extremely high neckline, it hung permanently on a hook behind her bedroom door. Cynthia thought it was horrid, but she didn't have the heart to get rid of it – it was a gift from her grandmother. It could have easily been a hand-me-down from the same.

I liked to tease Cynthia about it, and I tried to adopt the kind of tone I'd grown up hearing my uncles Morris and Kevin use on their wives. I'd pretend I didn't believe the grandmother story, insisting Cynthia had picked out the nightgown herself, at Zellers. Other times I'd encourage her to wear it, swearing it turned me on just to see it hanging there. "Imagine," I'd say in a lewdly suggestive tone, "if you actually *put it on*." This usually earned me a punch in the shoulder or chest.

After I heard the bathroom door close down the hall, I quickly stripped down to my underwear. Leaving my clothes in a pile at my feet, I threw the nightgown over my head. I had just enough time to thread my arms into the sleeves before Cynthia exited the bathroom. I pranced my way down the hall, toward her. When she saw me, she put a palm to her forehead. She shook her head and laughed. "You are a total wacko," she beamed.

I was in the middle of an elegant pirouette when the intercom rang.

Cynthia answered, and a man's voice crackled *chicken* through the speaker. Cynthia buzzed the lobby door open and I gathered the money. She put her hand out to take it from me but I walked right past her, down the hall toward the apartment door. "*I'll* get it," I called back, pretending to be insulted by her assumption.

"You wouldn't."

"I would. *You* may be ashamed of the nightgown, but I, for one, refuse to live a lie."

"You are completely insane."

"Hush," I scolded. I was really putting it on. "The only thing insane around here is how crazily comfortable this nightgown is."

It was actually true: it felt light as a bed sheet, more comfortable than I could have possibly imagined. And as I waited by the door for a knock, a broad smile formed on my face. A great feeling of warmth was about my shoulders and neck: the semester was nearly done, Christmas break was fast on the way, I had an awesome girlfriend (I practically lived with her!), and I was about to freak out a barbecue chicken deliveryman with some ridiculous ladies' sleepwear.

But when I opened the door, it was I who received a jolt.

My uncle, his hair greying now but still cropped short like in that old family photo, stood before me. In one hand, he clutched two cardboard boxes tied together with a string. In the other, a small brown paper bag. He looked me up and down; I saw him raise one eyebrow, briefly, but his face was otherwise expressionless. If my state of dress fazed him at all, he hid it very professionally. "That's going to be twelve sixty-six, please."

"Sidney?"

"Um. Yeah?"

"It's me," I said. "Robert. Bobby."

Sidney cocked his head and stared at me intently. "Bobby? Oh, wow!" He extended one arm as if to shake hands, but the food was in the way. Awkwardly, I took the boxes and the bag from him and pivoted to place them on the floor behind me. When I turned back to my uncle, he was scratching his chin and chuckling quietly. "Jeez, Bobby – does your mother know?"

It was one joke, just six words, but Sidney's delivery was so familiar it gave me a chill. The words were cutting, but the elocution was warm. Dropped into the same situation, either of my two other uncles would have said the exact same thing, in the exact same way.

I found myself, as I'd been doing nearly all my life, attempting to one-up one of my uncles with a joke. "Sure, she knows. She lent this thing to me." As usual, I found my effort wanting.

"Listen," Sidney said, pointing behind him with a thumb, "I've got other orders in the car. It's great to see you, but—"

"Of course," I said. "Here." I held out the money.

Sidney put up a hand. "No, no. It's on me."

"Really? Thanks." There was an uncomfortable pause. On impulse, I filled it. "Hey. We should get together some time."

"Oh, yeah, yeah," Sidney mumbled, backing away. I wasn't sure he meant it, but before turning the corner of the hallway, he said, "Come by the restaurant some time."

I closed the apartment door. I looked at the money in my hand – three blue fives. I figured I was owed at least as much.

Cynthia was standing at the end of the hall.

"What just happened?"

"It's a long story."

I filled Cynthia in on everything. I told her about the different dollar bills and my unfortunate choice when I was too young to know any better. I recounted my childhood assumptions and imaginings about my uncle's wealth. I told her about Sidney's absence from the extended family, about how no one ever talked about him, and about the strange way my mother acted when I brought up his name. Telling these little stories brought me immense pleasure. My heart beat a little faster in my chest and there was a tingly feeling about my ears. That Cynthia was fascinated by the whole affair only added to my fun. And while I was uncertain about what to do next, for her there was no question.

The following Friday, we set out for a late dinner at the chicken restaurant. It was a fifteen-minute walk from our building; I couldn't help but marvel at how, after so many years spent wondering and guessing about my uncle, I now lived in the same neighbourhood where he worked.

Cynthia and I stomped the snow from our boots in the restaurant entranceway and breathed in the hearty scent of French fries and barbecue. While the place looked clean, its décor appeared to have been last updated in the Seventies. We were greeted by a black pegboard sign on a simple metal pedestal, its white letters arranged to instruct us to wait to be seated. Hanging on a wall nearby was a framed review of the place, yellowed at the edges, clipped from a newspaper dated March 21, 1981. Dark wood strip panelling covered the walls. The floor was speckled black, grey, and murky white.

A waitress arrived to greet us. The burnt orange lipstick she wore almost matched the shade of the dye in her hair. She had a wrinkled face but moved about with vitality. After saying hello, she nimbly pivoted on one foot and, over her shoulder, asked us to follow her to a table. She led us through the dining area to a booth with cushy burgundy vinyl seats. The menu was printed on paper placemats already laid on the table. In the tiled ceiling above our heads, circular patterns of perforations pumped out elevator music.

The waitress left us to peruse our placemat menus. Cynthia stared at me, an expectant look on her face. I knew she wanted me to ask for Sidney, but I was having second thoughts. After years of curiosity, I couldn't help but wonder if I was now invading my uncle's privacy. The waitress returned with two small glasses of water.

"Is Sidney working tonight?" Cynthia asked her.

I felt my face redden.

Cynthia pointed at me. "That's his nephew."

"You don't say." The waitress leaned one hand on our table and stared at me for an uncomfortably long time. "Oh, I see it," she said, finally. "Definitely. I think it's the nose. Does everyone in your family have that nose?"

I couldn't help but place a finger on the tip of my nose. "I'm not really sure."

"Sid's out on a delivery now," the waitress said, "but I'll send him over as soon as he gets back."

When we were alone again, I balled up my paper napkin and threw it at Cynthia. "Thanks a whole lot."

She smiled mischievously. "I've always liked your nose."

"I don't doubt it," I answered, feigning annoyance.

"Shut up and enjoy the tunes," she said, glancing up at the ceiling. A soft keyboard rendition of "I Can't Go for That (No Can Do)" by Hall & Oates was playing. Swaying to the beat, Cynthia provided the vocals.

She knew every word.

We were eating when Sidney emerged from the kitchen and approached our table. On her side of the booth, Cynthia scooted over to the wall, making room, offering him a seat. I introduced my uncle to my girlfriend.

"So, were those your pajamas Bobby was wearing the other day?"

"Mine, yes," Cynthia laughed, already charmed, "but I swear, I never wear that thing."

"Of course you don't," Sidney returned, "if he always is."

We chatted for a while, mostly small talk. Sidney had been delivering for the chicken restaurant for about four years; before that he'd had work – he didn't specify what kind – up at Mirabel Airport. I asked him how long he had worked for the alarm company. He looked confused. "Alarm company?" I told him the last time I'd seen him, he'd been installing alarms up in Montclair. "Oh, yeah," Sidney said in a faraway tone. "Not for very long," he offered.

Cynthia, bless her, tried to steer the conversation in a more meaningful direction, but Sidney was evasive.

"So. You're Rob's mother's brother?"

"Yeah, but *he* can tell you that."

A man in a gravy-stained apron appeared in the kitchen door-way and waved at Sidney.

"Gotta go. Delivery time."

Just then Cynthia began to hop up and down in her seat, a look of pure joy on her face. Sidney, who had slid out of the booth, stared at her, intrigued. I wondered what could have been causing her to act so delighted, so suddenly. When our eyes met, she pointed at the ceiling. Then she began to sing. *Suzanne takes you down to her place near the river.*

Sidney turned to me, puzzled.

"She's crazy for Leonard Cohen."

"Really?" Sidney angled an ear toward the ceiling. Then he brightened. "I deliver to Leonard Cohen sometimes, you know."

"Come on," Cynthia said.

"Yeah, yeah. It's true. He calls once or twice a week. He gets the Half-Chicken Dinner. With extra sauce."

A picture appeared in my head: Leonard Cohen sitting on a couch, a paper napkin tucked into his collar like a bib, stooped over a takeout box of chicken on a coffee table, greasy fingers dipping French fries into one of two Styrofoam containers of barbecue sauce. It seemed totally ridiculous.

"Oh my god," Cynthia said. "That's *unbelievable.*"

"You really like Leonard Cohen?" Sidney asked, sounding skeptical.

"Like him? I *love* him. There's no one better."

Sidney sat back down in the booth and leaned over the table, drawing our heads nearer to his. He turned and peeked over his shoulder in the direction of the kitchen. Then he turned back to us. In a hushed tone, he said to Cynthia, "You should come with me, the next time Cohen calls. You can bring him his order." Then, looking only at me, he winked.

"Are you crazy?" Cynthia said. "I'd be so nervous I'd barf."

"Okay," Sidney sang. "If you don't want to meet him—"

"I'll do it!" Cynthia said. Then she grabbed my hands across the table. "But you have to come with me."

"I wouldn't miss it."

When I told my mother I had made contact with Sidney, she responded with silence.

"Hello?" I said into the telephone receiver.

"Hello," she replied, monotone.

"Is something wrong?"

"What do you want to go and get involved with *him* for?"

Now it was my turn to be silent; I didn't know what to say.

"What right does he have to even *talk* to you?"

"I don't know, maybe because of the fact that we're *related*?"

"Related," she spat. "Big deal. Everything was fine the way it was. You don't need him in your life. You didn't need to go and find him."

"Mom. I didn't go on some big quest to find him. It's like I told you: I ordered chicken, he delivered it."

"So stop ordering chicken."

"I really don't get it, Mom. What is your problem with Sidney?"

"*My* problem?" She sounded enraged. "Who says *I* have a problem?"

"Okay, okay," I said. "I'm not saying you have a problem. It's only a figure of speech. What is *the* problem? What is *the* problem with Sidney?"

She didn't answer me right away. I waited for her. "He's a strange bird," she said. Quickly, she added, "And that's all there is to it. Are you coming up this weekend?"

Her attempt to change the subject was a cue, and I let the matter go. My appetite for provoking my mother was not as strong as it had once been.

When I hung up, I noticed that the fingers of my left hand, the hand that I hadn't been holding the phone with, were clamped across the middle of my palm. I relaxed my grip. Four short lines, indentations, marked the spots where my fingernails had been digging into my skin.

Sidney's call came two weeks later. Cynthia's excitement was palpable. We jogged up to Sherbrooke Street, slipping on the slick sidewalk, laughing. In the cold air, our breath came out like steam. It was the same colour as the pale grey sky overhead. When Sidney pulled up in his car, I let Cynthia get in the front seat. I crawled into the back, next to a stack of takeout meals. The interior of my uncle's car had the same warm and succulent barbecue scent to it that the restaurant did; the tree-shaped air freshener hanging from his rear-view mirror was superfluous. Sidney did a U-turn in the middle of the intersection and we headed west.

Cynthia didn't think to put her seatbelt on until we were stopped at a red light.

We parked in front of an apartment building on Sherbrooke near the corner of Walkley. After we all got out of the car, Sidney handed me two fives and a ten, plus a handful of coins, to make change with. He also passed me a brown paper bag filled with utensils, napkins, and a container of coleslaw. Then, holding the cardboard box by the string that was wrapped around it, he presented Leonard Cohen's Half-Chicken Dinner to Cynthia. She took it with both palms upturned, beneath the box. She winced – it was hot to the touch.

Sidney made a clicking sound with his tongue. "Here." He pinched the string with his fingers again and lifted the box from Cynthia's hands. "You're supposed to hold it by the string."

"Good to know," Cynthia said, with humour in her voice. She cleared her throat. Her cheeks were flushed and she blinked a few times in rapid succession. She took the box back in the prescribed manner, dangling it away from her body.

"Find his name on the board and call him on the intercom," Sidney instructed. Cynthia nodded and turned toward the building. I followed her, and when I passed my uncle our eyes met. He gave me a wink.

Of course, I could have stopped it all right then.

But I was feeling too important; there was a glow about me that I was enjoying too much, the satisfaction of being in cahoots with one of my uncles was too enchanting.

I could say that I didn't know what was going to happen (or – perhaps more believably – that it was only in that very moment, with that particular wink, that I began to wonder if something was up), but that would be a lie. Because I knew. Of course I knew. My uncle's wink outside the apartment building was merely confirmation of what I'd known, deep down, all along. Because this is what men in my family do. With a chuckle that sounds warm, and with a knowing, well-timed (and well-aimed) wink, we tease, belittle, and trivialize the women in our lives. This was our entertainment. *They* were our entertainment.

The directory on the wall in the lobby of the building had two columns of names inside tiny rectangular windows. There was a little round button beside each name. Halfway down the first column, we found *Leonard Cohen*, written, like all of the other names, in scraggly cursive on sun-bleached paper. Cynthia bit her bottom lip and rang Leonard Cohen's bell.

The intercom clicked. Barely above a whisper, a man's voice purred, "Yes?" Maybe in that moment Cynthia pictured Leonard Cohen's face; maybe she imagined that his eyes were only half open and that his lips were but a centimetre from the microphone on his end. She took a step back, her eyes wide, and stared at the intercom. I looked at her and cocked my head toward the speaker, urging her to say something. She shook her head, terrified. The voice came through the speaker again, now sounding irritated. "Hello?"

"Um," I began. "Chicken?"

Cynthia and I climbed two flights of stairs and made our way down a brown-carpeted hallway with white stuccoed walls. An apartment door at the end of the hall opened at the same time that we arrived in front of it.

A grizzled old man stood in the doorway with a fistful of five-dollar bills. He wore a billowing yellow cardigan, unbuttoned, atop a pea green polo shirt. His plaid pants, two shades of brown, were held up by a belt with a Donald Duck buckle. His wispy white hair was longish on the top and brushed precariously across his scalp, turning up slightly at the ends. It looked like the slightest draft would have dislodged it. The old man waved his money with one hand and gestured at the food with the other.

He was a terrible tipper.

When the apartment door closed again, my heart was still racing from the thrill of the prank, of the betrayal. There was a sort of ecstasy, too – ecstasy laced with just the slightest inkling of nausea. I smiled expectantly at Cynthia, the way you smile at someone right after they've opened your Christmas present. She was scowling, her face bright red. "Your uncle is a total jackass."

"Well," I laughed, "that *was* Leonard Cohen. That was *a* Leonard Cohen."

Her expression changed from anger to one of disbelief. "Did you know?"

I hesitated to answer. I tried to contain the smile Cynthia's question had prompted. I tried to dull the twinkle it must have brought to my eye.

She stormed past me, twisting her torso so that her back was flush with the wall in the hallway. No part of her body touched mine.

I jogged after her down the hall and down the stairs, calling her name, but Cynthia wouldn't stop, wouldn't look back. She punched the door to the lobby open, and did the same to the door to the outside.

Sidney was waiting for us down on the sidewalk, arms crossed, leaning his back against the passenger side of his car. With a big satisfied smile on his face, he watched Cynthia approach his position. When she marched right by him, he called out to her back. "Hey, how about if next week you help me deliver to Pierre Trudeau? He lives on Benny Crescent and he gets the Double Leg Special!" Cynthia stopped at the tail end of Sidney's car. She swivelled, and pounded the trunk with the base of her fist. Sidney ducked, feigning shock, and curled both of his forearms over his head, as if an explosion had gone off beside him.

Cynthia took no notice of this. She was already walking swiftly away from us.

Sidney straightened. Steam billowed from his mouth and nostrils as he chuckled to himself. He looked at me and, again, winked. His gesture expressed warmth for me, but somehow it didn't feel like it was coming from a familial connection, from the fondness of an uncle for a nephew. The feeling of connection that I was getting from Sidney came from a different place altogether. It came from both of us being men.

I had one foot pointed toward Cynthia, who was growing smaller and smaller in my vision, and the other pointed toward my uncle, the man I had so many questions for, the man I had desperately wanted in my life for as long as I could remember.

"Not the sharpest tool in the shed, is she?"

"Pardon?" A cold sensation washed over my chest.

"Her. What's her name – Cindy? She fell for that one easily enough, didn't she?"

"Um. I think I better—" I pointed in Cynthia's direction.

"Yeah, you better. You better or you'll be sleeping on the couch for who knows how long. What're you gonna do, eh? Girls."

All I could bring myself to do was look at my uncle and shrug.

Cynthia had much to say to me. When I opened my mouth to speak, she shut me up before I could utter a word. She said she would tell me when it would be time for me to talk. I thought, *fair enough*.

I never told my mother about the Leonard Cohen stunt. And she never asked me about Sidney again. It was easier that way, I think, for both of us.

In the spring, I found myself passing by Sidney's restaurant. I had no intention of stopping, but the waitress who had served Cynthia and me back in December was in the big window of the place, wiping the glass. She waved me inside.

"Could have sworn you were Sid when I saw you coming down the street. A sight for sore eyes that would have been, eh?" She laughed.

I tried to process the waitress's words.

"Where's he gone, anyway?" she asked with genuine curiosity and a hint of concern. "He didn't tell anyone when he quit."

I didn't know what to say. I considered inventing something – a new job, maybe a new town – just to keep up appearances. I considered admitting my ignorance, appearances be damned.

I dithered long enough to provide the waitress with an answer.

"He didn't tell you, either," she marvelled. She shook her head and let out a little laugh. "What a guy."

The news that my uncle had moved on from the restaurant did not surprise me. A part of me, on a level barely detectable, had expected it. The only thing I felt about this development was relief. My uncle Sidney was absent, his whereabouts were unknown, and the date of his next appearance – if there ever was to be one – was uncertain. This was the man I had always known.

Before leaving the restaurant, I ordered a family-size French fry to go. I took it back to the apartment to share with Cynthia. She'd be home soon.

Christine Miscione

YOUR FAILING HEART.

The nurse says she is sorry, and it clings to the air, to every atom, to every speck of dust and trace of antiseptic. The nurse says she is sorry and that I can take my time, take as long as I need, then she hands you to me; you're finally in my arms and I feel the weight of the world while I hold you. I think of how strange it is that you are outside me, that you have endings, and here you are, so compact and small and all of you contained behind skin. I think of how this must be what it felt like to travel before photographs – to have only faith because there is no tangible proof, and how even blind faith can never prepare you for the moment of arrival, for this skin of yours which holds all of you so tightly, that I made, that I struggled to imagine, having made it without wanting to. Here you are in my arms and I can study you, your pink translucence swaddled tightly in baby blue linen, your chubby neck and head and flaming Celtic red hair – you look nothing like me. Your plump cheeks, your white lashes curled tightly like fringe around your eyes, which are pressed closed but not too hard. It is like you are only sleeping.

In the summers of my childhood, my Nonna rented a vegetable plot from a community garden inside an aviary. Dressed in widow's black, she'd work the land beneath fierce sun while I'd trudge through the thick May grass under Japanese crabapples, the perfume of their cherry-pink blossoms catching wind off the lake. I'd stalk snails near the algae-green ponds and Ozymandian sculptures. I'd taunt the parrots behind their wire cages, hoping for a hello. I'd nap in the pools of shade made when the late-day sun finally tilted over the cedar hedges. Running between the garden plots and cages of birds, my heart was buoyant and the afternoons endless. I would've told you to hold onto those moments as long as you could. I would have said to you, don't let your heart wish for anything else.

It was the spring before my eleventh birthday that I finally climbed into that massive cedar hedge bounding the aviary. I discovered sections hollowed of branches, secret rooms spread out before my eyes, furnished with stumps for chairs, nooks filled with rusting treasures left behind by neighbourhood kids. I saw a manual Rototiller wedged between two spindly branches, its sharp metal teeth spotted with rust. I thought, wouldn't it be a good idea to forge ahead and build another room, where I could consort with cicadas in June and those tiny toads in mid-summer. I loosened the tiller from between the branches and was about to take it into my arms like a warrior goddess, when I tripped in a deep indentation in the sandy dirt and fell forward, impaling my shoulder on two of its blades.

I remember that day, lurching towards Nonna's plot, blood pouring down my chest, my face hot with tears. She looked up casually from where she was digging out a lettuce plant gone to seed. She shook her head. Nonna, with her cross affixed to her chest. Nonna, with her eternal widow's black, fifteen years after Nonno's death. Her wartime sensibility, her cold sadness, her callused hands pressing a rag into my gushing shoulder while she dragged me bloody to the car. She kept shaking her head and finally said, in broken English, I told you to be careful. The peacocks watched from their cages, their feathers fanned for mating. I told you to be careful, she repeated, then repeated again eight years later, last August, when the soggy spring grass had receded and dried under the swelter of late-summer. Last August when Franc and I were saving ourselves, eighteen-years-old, and the afternoons felt endless again. Last August, Nonna looked up from the television and said, I told you to be careful. This time I stumbled bloody into her living room, my underwear torn and soaked.

When Franc comes to visit the hospital later today, when he sees you, he and I will look at each other like, now what? Nothing is as we imagined. Months ago, Franc said he would never stop loving me but that we couldn't be together because of what I chose. Franc said it was too painful, there was still so much love and my belly was growing. When he comes today he will probably bring some flowers and something tiny for you. He doesn't know yet. Then he will look from you to me with tears in his eyes. Now what? Except now we have the knowledge of each other's limits, the terms and conditions of our love.

The May before last August was the wettest on record. The boggy grass around the garden plots in the aviary was almost neon green and yellow-tipped like an overwatered, over-loved houseplant. Franc and I were taking it slow, a seven-course meal, savouring every shoulder graze, each thrill of when our fingers, our hands, would find each other. It had just rained that afternoon and I could smell the fragrant cedar mulch and dank bird feed. Nonna had become too frail – her plot overtaken by dandelions and rogue oregano. I showed Franc anyway and described it as it used to be: divided neatly into rows of tomatoes and lettuces and herbs. Then I showed him the cedar hedge, that kingdom of childhood. We had to crouch to get inside. We sat on two stumps and laughed so hard we fell into our first kiss.

I know nothing of your father except his strong coarse hand pushing hard against my mouth. I know nothing except his head shaved to bare scalp, his thrust like a hammer pound, how it burned inside me when he came. He smelled like musky after-shave and his stubble scratched my cheeks. In the moonlight I caught only a glimpse of his face, his skin covered in freckles, tiny markings leftover from boyhood, and for the briefest second, he was human. Then, I must've been whimpering because he growled at me to shut up. He pinned my shoulders down with his forearm and dug his elbow into my old scar. This was your begin-ning. The moon was full that night, I remember, so bright and determined that when I tried to sleep, it wouldn't be contained. It seeped under my bedroom door, it glowed between the slits of my blinds. It drilled into my eyes, even with my eyelids pressed closed. From every angle I was exposed.

Nonna told me I should've been more careful. She refused to take me to the police because what did I think would happen if I wore my cut-off jean shorts and turquoise tank top at night? What did I think would happen if I took a shortcut from Franc's house that cut diagonally across town, cutting through the forested ravine beyond the aviary garden?

I finally told Franc three weeks later because I had stopped return-ing his phone calls and couldn't bear him thinking he did some-thing wrong. I thought for certain he'd see me as damaged, but he took me into his arms and I felt his tears against my cheeks. He kept saying it will be okay, everything will be okay. Then he told me he loved me for the first time.

I lied and told Franc I had already gone to the police. I lied and said I was over it. Then I told him about you and he reassured me and he said he'd bring me to the clinic to take care of it. To take care of you. I agreed and felt sure and it wasn't until I was trembling in the yellow clinic smock, until the doctor had introduced herself and showed me the cartoon of the uterus, that I finally realized I couldn't. But you're making the wrong choice, Franc pleaded. Don't you want to choose us, to choose me? I told him I was trying not to choose anything.

I secretly smoked cigarettes and ran hard every day of my first and second trimester. I soaked in water so hot it rivalled the core of the earth. I ate cold cuts and runny eggs and canned tuna. It was only a month or so ago that the winter splintered into early spring, that my heart did the same. In the sudden spike of humidity, I couldn't sleep. I tossed and turned in my bed, desperate for the cool side of the pillow, the sheets. I turned so violently that I rolled straight off the bed. Rushing to the bathroom, crying, I checked with my fingers to see if there was blood. This was the moment I realized maybe I did want you.

We are at an impasse, Franc had told me a few months after that failed doctor's appointment. It was late November, those dark days when autumn droops into winter, when I was beginning to show. We stood in the aviary parking lot and I could hear the peacock crying. Franc said, I want you to prove your love by choosing me; you want me to prove my love by choosing you, but this situation is bigger than us. Then he gripped my back and I dug my face into his neck and it was like we were hanging onto the moment because we knew we would never have it again.

I chose you, not Franc. I chose you, not that other life coiled like a bulb in one of the aviary plots, bounding with possibility. I chose you and now look at you, your eyes closed but not too hard; it is like you are only sleeping. I stick my index finger inside your tiny curled hand and you don't hold on. I kiss your cold forehead and hope for a gurgle but there's nothing. They say milk will come in a few days. What will happen to it now? I chose you and you didn't keep your end of the deal. I chose you and the nurse said she was sorry and it's still there, heavy and present, as heavy and present as the dark to a dog that attacks it. Maybe it's better this way. You'll never have to think how I couldn't walk properly for days, or sleep for months, or how I couldn't look Franc in the eyes and tell him I love him back. You'll never have to wonder if you are like your father – except, how could you have been anything like him? That shadow in the night who gave you to me.

I chose you, my sweet little one. But life didn't give us each other.

Lorna Crozier

REBOOTING EDEN

"I've got the problem solved," he said. He put down the news-paper and removed his reading glasses so he could see her better. "We'll plant the back garden with fruit trees."

"Why would we do that?" she said. "Fruit trees are a lot of trouble." He looked fragile to her without his glasses. For one thing, his bad eye, the one with the worst glaucoma, teared up, the lids puffy, the skin underneath slightly inflamed. You noticed it less when he wore his glasses. You noticed less too the nakedness of his face and head. Since he'd shaved off his beard and mous-tache just a month ago, there was no interruption in the broad expanse of pale flesh from chin to crown.

On a bald man, she thought, glasses are like a fence that breaks up the monotony of an immense lawn. In her case, a woman whose hair remained substantial, her specs performed a different function: they detracted from the wrinkles and tiredness around her eyes. She didn't bother wearing eye makeup any more. Ten years ago she wouldn't have gone out the door, even for a quick trip to the corner grocer's, without mascara.

It was one of the many things that had changed. She could make a list of them, she'd recently told the younger of their two middle-aged daughters, a list long enough to climb one wall of their living room, cross the ceiling, and go down the other side.

For weeks they'd been trying to figure out ways they could stay in the house. The garden out back was becoming too much for them, though last fall they'd replaced some of the flowers with shrubs. The better part of each day was taken up with staking and weeding and deadheading and watering. They loved doing it, they kept saying, and they meant it, at least she did, and she wanted to believe her husband's dogged claims. If they didn't garden, what would they do instead?

Even retired academics like them, people who'd spent most of their lives rolling in the stink of books, could read for only so long. After a couple of hours she could feel herself stumbling through the sentences, bestseller escape fiction no exception, as if she were trying to follow some strange language she barely remembered. They'd agreed daytime television was a no-no. Once you got into the odd half-hour program to punctuate your day there was no stopping the cooking shows, the renovation nightmares, the bossy judges and Dr. Phils who were so sure of everything. And the other common way their job-free acquaintances passed the time – volunteering? "It smacks of amateurism," he said.

"And who wants to do for nothing what you used to do for money?" she added. Teaching new immigrants English, for example, or doing the odd bit of editing for a community magazine, or raising the literacy level of the high-school boy who delivered flyers on his bike and who addressed them as "youse guys."

"It would be worse than marking first-year essays," her husband said, something they had loathed more and more each year. They sounded snobby, she knew. They sounded terrible. They'd never say these things around their younger offspring, who, in her early forties, seemed to value political correctness above all things. Maybe they had too when they were younger. But wasn't there something to be said for honesty? There wasn't enough time left to pretend you were nicer than you really were.

The garden, they'd assured themselves more than once, was their salvation. For the past two decades it had kept them alert and fit – she still admired his biceps when he wore a T-shirt – but they were almost eighty. How much longer could they keep up that strenuous backyard labour? Their property was not a narrow city lot; it was close to half an acre. And coastal gardening didn't stop for winter. There was a pause, a December and January stutter, and then the weeds invaded – God, how she hated scarlet pimpernel – and the lettuce seeds, as small as flyspecks on a windowpane, needed to be planted in the cold frame.

"You're already stooped like your father," she said. "And I can hear my knees grinding when I bend. How long can we go on?" When he didn't respond, she was going to repeat herself, more loudly this time in case he'd turned down his hearing aids, but then he said, "You know those two apple trees in the side yard? How much time do you spend on them?"

"Not a lot."

"Nothing really. All you do is pick the apples." He dabbed at his eye with the small hanky he kept in the shirt pocket where he'd once stashed cigarettes. A drawer of hankies had been part of his mother's estate, and for some reason, which was now clear, he hadn't thrown them out. Thank God he'd stopped smoking five years ago. She thought he'd quit for her, but he told her later that his lungs had started aching and he'd felt death was kneeling on his chest when he lay down. He'd been scared. There'd been a pain around his heart. Well, fear could be a good teacher when love didn't work. She decided to keep that thought to herself – he didn't need to hear it.

"My point exactly," she said. "It's a lot of work picking anything when it gets ripe all at once. For months you'd die for a fig or a ripe plum and then suddenly you're bombarded. Already the blueberries wear us out." She started loading the dishwasher. "We won't want to do it. And if you think for one moment I'm going to can or make jam like I used to, think again."

She closed the door of the dishwasher with a firm push. He'd get to it later, putting the cutlery handle-side down when she wanted it handle-side up. This was one of the things he did that drove her crazy. The meticulousness he'd shown as a scholar had morphed into annoying domestic tics. If she set down her book to go to the bathroom, when she returned, it was gone. He'd put it back on one of their many bookshelves where she couldn't easily find it though he insisted on the logic of the alphabet. To keep the fridge tidy enough for his exacting standards, he'd add the leftovers from the previous meal to the chicken and wine stew she had bubbling on the stove without asking her if it was okay. His additions sometimes ruined the whole dish. He'd never admit it.

Now he was spraying the granite counter with vinegar and water though she'd just wiped it clean with a cloth. "But we won't even have to pick the fruit," he said. "We can phone a service that provides healthy food for the indigent and they'll harvest the trees and give everything away. We won't have to do a damned thing and we'll be helping others out."

"And where do you find a service like that?"

"I read about it in the paper."

She was leery about what he discovered in the paper. In the past it had gotten them into trouble. Like the health column that claimed vitamin A prevents colds and slows down Alzheimer's. He ordered the supplements and got them on a high dose, 10,000 units if she remembered correctly. What little hair that had remained bravely attached to his head ended up on his pillow in the morning, and her skin, once so luminous, turned the yellow of the collar of her favourite white blouse, lost then found in the bottom of a drawer. They became inordinately irritable, flying off the handle at the least annoyance. After questioning them both about changes in their diet, their doctor figured out the culprit and sternly warned them about messing with vitamin miracles that could be as toxic as Laetrile.

Because of a report in last month's paper, he'd tossed out their dental floss. The latest studies deemed it was ineffective. While they watched the late-night news they poked at their gums and dug between their teeth with toothpicks. "They don't make them like they used to," he said. Too many of them splintered in the spaces between the incisors and she worried there'd be slivers in her gums. Floss seemed elegant in comparison.

As they picked away, flicking out bits of meat and green beans, she wondered how they'd ended up here, two people in their golden years – ha! – obsessed with dental hygiene, settled on side-by-side twin reclining chairs that raised and lowered with the push of a button, their calves and muffled feet elevated on the footrests. "In these sheepskin slippers our feet look like altar offerings to a minor god," she said, muting the television so he'd hear. "What would you name *that* deity?"

"God of Domestic Torpor," he said. She loved being the straight man to his cleverness. Their repartee, in the days when they had the energy to go out two, maybe three, times a week, had made them popular as dinner guests.

Fifty years ago – was it really half a century? – they'd met at a conference on medieval studies in Dijon. After hearing each other's papers, brilliant, just brilliant, and spending the next three days in his better-than-her hotel room, they went home to their marriages and tenured-track professorships in different cities and, within the week, as classes were about to begin, they left their jobs and spouses.

Nothing had topped it for daring in the decades since. And looking at her husband now, dabbing at his weepy eye with his mother's hankie, a gesture that prompted both sadness and tenderness to flutter in her belly, she could say, in all honesty, even factoring in his quirks and small obsessions, she didn't regret it.

The scandal of their adultery – how titillating it had been, how it had fired every cell in her lower body – forced them to move to another town and a smaller college that took a chance on them as a pair. That was a rare thing in those days, and she'd have been out of luck if they'd been in the same department. Usually the man got the job and the woman didn't, no matter what her scholarly achievements. According to their colleagues who refused to retire ("Will they teach till they drool?" he asked), spousal hiring was now part of the contract for new faculty, and day care was steps away from the campus office buildings.

The college that took them on was not going to fan the flames of their academic reputations. Their salaries plummeted. But at least it was on Vancouver Island, not in northern Ontario or rural Manitoba, and they still got funding to go to Dijon and Florence and Barcelona, places that had nothing to do with the themes of the annual conferences or the papers they delivered. They stayed in lovely hotels in the oldest quarters of the cities, that sepia European light spilling through cranky windows over their sleeping bodies where the top sheet had slipped away.

If she'd been a painter, she'd have tried to capture that scene. Sometimes she saw them young and naked, before their daughters were born, wrapped around each other in an endless afternoon, as if she'd drifted out of her physical self and looked down from some gilded ancient ceiling.

Their scholarly findings, hers on the influence of *milles fleurs* tapestries on contemporary garden practices, his on medieval war hammers and their double function as instruments of construction and death, were presented to a handful of people, most of them hungover from the cocktail hour and wine-soaked dinner the evening before. There was an unspoken agreement she remembered well: I'll attend your session if you attend mine.

Was there a time when they believed their findings would change the world, would make a difference to even one living human being? It was odd they'd never discussed this. She'd have to ask him on their walk tonight. Someone, she thought, should research the effect of pedestrian peregrinations on the depth and honesty of a conversation. When they strolled around the block after dinner, they were more candid, more daring than when they sat across from each other at the table. Was that because they looked at the ground instead of at each other's faces? she wondered. They had to be careful where they placed their feet so they wouldn't fall.

When they stopped teaching, they rarely travelled. After those decades of funding, it seemed odd, unfair really, to spend their own money on tickets and accommodation, and once they'd sorted through their files and cleaned out the shelves in their department offices, their subjects and the European sites they'd intellectually plundered for new material held little appeal.

In their response to the Chair's toast at their retirement party, he quipped that he'd be surrendering his war hammers for spades and trowels and shovels. And the *milles fleurs* of her tapestries were already rising, she claimed in her short reply, like pollen from the cloth to become the dozens of floral varieties in their garden.

"I'd like to see the newspaper article," she said, "where they talk about this fruit-picking group. What's it called?" They were in the backyard, which seemed to be expanding every day as their height – they were measured every year in the doctor's office – shrunk. Each had lost close to three inches: she was now five foot six and he just under six feet. Hunched over the shovel, turning over the soil where they'd harvested the garlic, he looked even shorter.

She sliced open bags of chicken manure with a sharp blade and shook it over the earth. It was one of the few garden smells she loathed, though the horticultural guru who wrote the weekly local column called its odour "sweet."

The first time her husband had followed the column's advice, he'd brought home bags of the stuff sold by the side of the road for half the going price. She knew now she should have questioned the bargain. It turned out the dusty contents were uncured. The droppings hadn't cooked in their own heat for long enough to destroy any damaging bacteria. Though the manure burned the lettuce plants and the leaves of the New Zealand spinach, they ate, on his insistence, what they could salvage. It was pure luck neither of them had come down with some terrible chicken virus.

When it started to rain, he leaned the wheelbarrow against the fence so it wouldn't fill with water, and she gathered their tools and gloves and put them in the shed. How she welcomed this change in the weather. As the first drops fell, she turned her face to the sky and opened her mouth like a naked bird waiting for its mother. There had been two months of drought.

Imagine – drought in a rain forest. Some days she was glad they wouldn't be around to see what would happen twenty years from now. No matter how well they watered the plants, nothing could beat even the smallest rain.

"I didn't know you'd taken a pill today," she said. She'd just come in with the laundry she'd rescued from the clothes line. Their avoidance of the dryer on sunny days was one of the ways they minimized their dependence on electricity. He was already in bed, waiting for her.

"Thought I'd surprise you." It was unusual for their love-making to be unplanned. There was his pill, which he had to take at least two hours before, and there was her estrogen suppository and Astroglide – the name made her think she was lubricating for some voyage into outer space – and before anything could happen, there were the images streaming on the laptop computer they'd set up on the dresser.

He'd found the video on the site, "Naked Girls: 10,000 Porn Movies Online." As she slipped out of her clothes, their favourite clip was running on mute. He'd pause it before it got to the part they liked, the male hero she'd nicknamed Dwayne (the name she hadn't come across since childhood seemed to capture his slicked back hair and boxy chin) catching the naked woman in the grove, pushing her against a tree, and banging into her while she fought, then moaned and dissolved into noisy ecstasy. She couldn't help but wonder if the young woman's back was scraped raw by the tree bark.

It was amazing, she reflected, how little of the scene they needed to get ready for each other. The lovemaking was fast too. When he could come, he came, often outside her. She passed him some Kleenexes and then he stroked her into orgasm – she could feel her clitoris jumping like a startled frog under his skillful finger. "Dwayne, Dwayne, Dwayne," she said in a whisper he couldn't hear. His hearing aids on his bedside table whined a single high-pitched note like strange cicadas if he put them too close together.

The film was sexist, slightly misogynistic, she'd admit, but tame and charmingly old-fashioned compared to some of the other clips they'd watched. Still, she didn't doubt their daughters would be shocked by the computer's contents if their parents perished in tandem, in bed or not. Erasing the file upon their deaths wasn't something they'd discussed with their lawyer, and she'd vetoed his suggestion that she ask a friend. They were of an age where you didn't reveal your manners in bed, as the American poet put it. And most of their friends no longer had a love life, as far as she could tell.

She understood their peers' surrender to celibacy. It took some courage to accept this too, too *un*solid flesh as one's own.

Lately when she undressed in front of him, she slipped between the sheets as quickly as a modest virgin. The odd time when they stayed in a hotel – and hotel sex continued to be better, more risqué than what they shared at home – she avoided the mirrors. "Are all interior designers young and buff?" she said out loud.

Every bathroom shocked you with a floor-to-ceiling reflection of what you looked like as you exited the tub: breasts flat and long as the ears of a basset hound; belly swaying like a bag of suet hanging from a branch; ample thighs dimpling. Even her labia drooped. And they were more visible. Her pubic hair had evaporated along with her vaginal moisture.

Aware that she was being selfish, she was relieved that his eyesight was bad. Maybe that was why she continued to be – though she bore no resemblance to the firm-bodied, sexually acrobatic academic he'd fallen in love with – the object of his desire. It broke her heart a little to think that his eyes, dim as they were, were the last that would ever find her beautiful.

As for his continuing allure for her? His custard-like belly, his flabby chest, his toenails tough and yellow as the claws of a bird of prey. "Women are less fussy" – she'd heard this said so many times, and she agreed. If a man was good company, if he cooked and cleaned and separated the clothes properly for the washing machine, if he comparison shopped for groceries and enjoyed it, his attractiveness ratio scooted upward.

Besides, though her friends had always found him handsome, it was his mind she'd fallen for when they'd met. It moved as lightly and quickly as a water spider over any topic, dipping in and out. Though forgetful, he'd never lost his brilliance and he could make her laugh. So, smartness, a good sense of humour, and a willingness to clean. Would these be the only essentials on her list if she went on one of those dating sites her widowed friends talked about? No mention of height, weight, or age limit? No mention of income-earning potential? "Lucky men," pops into her head a dozen times a day, and sometimes it slips out, though usually he doesn't hear.

He'd figured out a quotient that explained the sexual tepidness of their friends: the more you doted on your grandchildren, dropping everything to babysit, flashing countless pictures on your cell phone, driving them to day care, soccer, etc., etc., the less interested you were in carnality. "I'm sure," he said, "there's a graduate student in gerontology writing a paper about the correlation right now. We'll volunteer to be research subjects." He grinned at her across the pillows. "Maybe we can get funding. We'll go to Amsterdam."

They loved their second daughter's children, who lived close by, they said this to each other daily, "We love those kids," but the two boys, ten and twelve, had never stayed overnight. If the family came for lunch, she served hot dogs or chicken fingers and chips. They both watched as the children built the new Lego monster she'd bought at Buddy's Toys for the occasion and chatted amicably as if there was nothing she and he would rather do. But the family – to be honest she thought of them as "the visitors" – left by mid-afternoon. "Nap time for us," he'd say, tapping the face of his watch if their daughter, her optometrist husband, and the kids had settled in. If only they'd known what "nap time" meant. "Hello, Dwayne," she whispered.

The society that gathered fruit for the poor was called "Resurrecting Eden." She found the name pretentious, but he phoned the number in the paper anyway. "They sound legitimate," he said. They'd send someone to pick the apples on the two trees ready for harvesting and that same person would help them draft future plans for the property. "If it's designated as a 'Resurrecting Eden Site'," he explained, "we'll become *la-di-da* hobbyists. Others will do the heaving and ho-ing."

Two days later, they'd hung a sign on the front door: "Come through the gate. We're in the garden." She was clipping back the asparagus ferns and he, with a long-handled net, was cleaning out the fall detritus that floated on the pond.

The young man who found them in the back was about five inches taller than her husband used to be. Did the height that disappeared from people like them end up on someone like him? Didn't the new physics say that nothing disappeared? She bet a lot of people, when they saw this gangly gardener towering above them, brought up dipsey doos and double dribbling and long dunk hang time. She could rattle off the jargon – every June she watched the NBA playoffs on TV with the excitement of a girl who'd excelled at the game in high school – but she resisted the temptation to tease him. Too much of life was insipid cleverness and cliché. That wasn't something she wanted to fall into.

"Hi," he said. "My name is Darryl." He shouted his introduction – the neighbours on either side would know his name now too. She could picture him and his ilk in their training sessions; they'd be told to speak to the elderly in a loud clear voice.

He wore a white short-sleeved shirt with "Resurrecting Eden" embroidered in red on the single pocket and shorts like the ones her optometrist son-in-law found in Walmart. His long, pale legs were fuzzed with reddish-brown hair. A clump of the same colour sat like a piece of turf on his head. When she talked about him later on their evening walk, she'd say he was the kind of man who wouldn't go bald. Some were just born lucky.

"Who came up with the word *Resurrecting*?" she'd asked the morning before as she waited for the toast to pop. "What do they think they're raising from the dead?" If she didn't stand guard at the counter, her husband would nab the toast and slap on a thick smear of butter. She used less than a teaspoon for both slices when she got to them first. Anything to stop his arteries from clogging up.

"Are the young even aware of the mythology? Remember how little our students knew."

"Wouldn't 'Rebooting Eden' have been a more fitting name for this age bracket?" she said. Perhaps in the new resuscitated version Adam and Eve would stay in the garden, they wouldn't grow old, they wouldn't toil until they dropped.

"Maybe," she said, "since this all has to do with picking fruit and giving it away, the only detail the founders of the group saved from the story was the apple." She must remember to ask her daughters and her grandchildren what Eden meant to them. Had there been a movie?

She'd left a wicker basket between the two trees but Darryl had a canvas bag on a strap slung over his shoulder. Darryl, she thought, a name very similar to Dwayne, equally as out of fashion, yet they were from different generations. The porn star, if still alive, could be Darryl's grandfather. Fancy that. A coincidence, of course, but they had the same stubborn chin.

She knew Darryl saw her as an old lady, which of course she was. His mouth curved upwards into that sappy, demented smile people his age beam on the elderly. She had to remind herself that it wasn't this tall young man's fault that she was doddering into an ever-shrinking future. It wasn't his fault that they needed help and he might be the one who could provide it. He carried a clipboard as if he were a coach in a training session. His team would never win, she thought, he'd forever come in third.

"So," Darryl shouted, sweeping his arm over the expanse of the back yard as if they needed sign language as well, "you've got quite the property here."

"Yeah," she said, "we fucking love it."

Her husband turned from the pond to look at her, a grin on his face. He lifted two fingers to the brim of his ball cap in a mock salute.

It was such an easy thing, really, to shock the young. It wasn't the word itself, of course, but the fact that it came from a deeply lined, white-haired woman older than his grandparents, if they were still alive. She felt ashamed for having sunk to such a tactic.

"Uh," Darryl stammered, "uh." He wouldn't meet her eyes.

And just at that moment, likely not because she'd said "fucking," not because of the beauty of the summer day or the label on Darryl's T-shirt, not because seven dragonflies needled the air above the marsh irises and the next-door terrier had started barking at the small disturbances in the galaxy of his grassy yard, not because the ice cream truck had stopped at their corner with the tune she assumed the three of them separately remembered from their childhoods, not because the message machine in the kitchen was recording their younger daughter asking if the grandsons could stay overnight because her husband had just left her and she couldn't be trusted to be a mother any more, not because a yellow warbler swayed on top of the bamboo that had finally grown high enough to block the neighbour's second-storey window from which they sometimes feared they were being watched, her husband of fifty years, the man who once knew more than anyone in the world about the constructive uses of medieval war hammers, tipped forward on the balls of his feet and fell rigid as a plank into the pond.

It was as if a meteor chunk had plummeted out of nowhere into the net he'd been holding and pulled him face down into the shallow water.

She leapt in. She thrashed through the water lilies and struggled to lift his heavy head and shoulders. "No," she cried. "No, no." She caught his glasses as they slipped from his face. Around them goldfish flickered like drenched candle flames, like something trying to stay lit in all that wet and cold.

She'd always known she'd be a widow. She could see the word written in invisible henna on every woman's forehead after she'd turned sixty if she was still living with a man. If she was blessed enough to be living with a man she loved. Every year it moved closer to the surface until it flashed like a neon sign.

Darryl had been the one to call 911, to help her raise him from the pond, to lay him on the deck and do CPR until the first responders arrived. How much time had passed, her husband's sopping head in her lap…ten minutes? Half an hour? An afternoon?

She climbed into the ambulance as if her legs were encased in cement, a young woman in a uniform boosting her up and into the back. Darryl stood there, drenched and awkward, his face stricken.

It baffled her, this need to say something to him in the few seconds before the ambulance closed its doors, maybe about their fondness for his grandfather – that is, the man she liked to think of as his grandfather. She wanted to hand him words as hard and solid as the apples he'd pack into his sack and later give away. Doubled over on the bench seat, she shivered in her wet clothes, though it was warm outside and a blanket had been draped across her shoulders. Beside her lay her husband attached to tubes and wires, eyes shut, face slick and cold to her touch.

The door closed. On the other side of the tall bamboo bordering the yard, she heard the neighbour yelling at the dog who'd begun to howl along with the siren as the tires spat gravel along the length of the driveway and then turned right at the road taking them farther and farther away from the garden into a future she didn't want to meet. If she'd been a different kind of woman she thought, planting her feet more firmly on the floor of the ambulance so she wouldn't sway too far to the side as it turned the corner, she'd have thrown back her head and joined the dog in one long, loud lament.

Bruce Meyer

CANTIQUE
DE JEAN RACINE

The École Niedermeyer is tucked away in the fifteenth arrondisse-
ment where a web of streets with literary names – Rue Victor
Hugo, Rue Diderot – encircle it in a harmony of cultural allu-
sions. The new building is just as grey and formidable as the one
it replaced in the Sixties; yet behind those grey walls, some of the
greatest French music was created. This was the school where
Gabriel Fauré triumphed over every possible obstacle that his
teachers and their teachers put in his way to compose the
Cantique de Jean Racine.

I pause before the great oak doors of the École and listen to
the cadres of pianos, each vying for supremacy – the atonal, the
lyrically baroque, the *de profundis* struggle for the emergence of a
single tune. It all becomes a blur of sound. Every player wants to
be heard. Every note has somewhere to go. The sense of the beautiful, individual composition evaporates into a cacophony like
early morning rain beneath a grey Parisian sky. The city smells
dank even on a clear day. When it rains, the city breathes the
aroma of rain breaking through shafts of sunlight. The foist holds
onto the past, and the past in Paris never goes away.

Listen. Do you hear it? One of the pianos has gone missing in
action. Has the player given up? Art is a war, of sorts, where every
artist wants to be heard. That's what distinguishes an artist from a
mere piano player. The artist needs to compete. His final reply to

the competition is silence. Has he abandoned his piece? Now the other pianos are falling silent, one by one. It must be the hour and the practice studios are changing over from one student to another. The lyrical one is still going. Debussy, or is it Saint-Saëns? It is Saint-Saëns. The piece is "Le Cygne," set for piano.

A passing van drowns out the music, but at that instant, I stop, close my eyes, and complete the melodic line that has been broken by the truck. I can see a swan as if it has been painted by Monet. The graceful bird glides beneath the Japanese bridge among the water lilies at Giverny. It makes me wonder where music goes after it is heard. Words last but music always seems so momentary, so temporary. *Littera scripta manet,* as the Latin motto has it. The written word survives. But music? Where does used music find its afterlife?

Music just disappears until someone brings it to life again. Music is in direct competition with nature. Music is the patterns of sounds that would otherwise be random noises, yet music is also the purest expression of nature because it continually fades away. When it is beautiful and memorable, and the mind holds onto it, it is like light passing through glass.

I can read music and enjoy listening to music, but I am not, alas, a musician.

I have books to look at on my shelves. They gather dust, but once they come into the world, they don't have to compete to be heard. They are simply there, on the shelf, waiting patiently. They don't need an afterlife because they exist according to rules that have nothing to do with time or time signatures. Books are a fact of life unto themselves. But I love music for its frailty. It is the afterlife of music that has brought me to the École Niedermeyer today: to research the failure and the triumph of Gabriel Fauré, and to test the question about whether music has an afterlife.

The École still offers an annual competition, the Prix d'École Niedermeyer, a prize for the best new work by a student. I am here to search for the facts behind the award the year it was given to the second-best composition by a student because the judges refused to give the prize to the best. That decision may, arguably, have changed the course of French music. The prize I am researching raises many questions. How do you judge a piece of music, or any art for that matter, that is so far ahead of its time it grows in strength and beauty with each decade and needs to be heard again and again? How do you see into the future when you gaze at a musical score and say, *yes*, that is the one people will want to hear for more than a few months – that is one that will be heard a hundred lifetimes from now.

Someone just slammed his or her fist on the keyboard. I surmise it is the new twelve-tone player who replaced the Saint-Saëns enthusiast, but I am just guessing. It doesn't sound like part of the composition. It is not twelve tone. It is anger. An artist tries to push himself beyond his limits. He can see the barrier he must break. He tries and fails. Failure is what propels an artist. Awards and prizes just rub it in: if you win, you wonder if you can repeat the accomplishment; if you fail and you wonder what you did wrong, so like Einstein's definition of insanity, an artist just keeps competing and repeating the same action until he burns out.

The École Niedermeyer is the cradle of French music, the birthplace of almost every familiar French melody, save for "Le Marseillaise" and "Frère Jacques." The interior hallway is concrete and feels military; the old school that once stood here resembled a barracks. The grey walls echo with failure. I can feel it the moment I enter because the foyer, at least, is cold, concrete, and inscrutable in its modern brutalist appearance. I smile at the old desk clerk as I sit in the waiting area for the archivist to come and fetch me and take me to the stacks of boxes on the third floor where I will find the score I want to settle. Settling scores is what resides at the heart of prizes. The clerk does not smile back.

And what is the score? Picture a young pupil of keyboard composition. He's in a competitive place. The older students say he shouldn't be there. He's too young. His military style uniform, mandatory for students of his time, is baggy. His family cannot afford a better-fitting outfit. "Young man in a hurry," his teachers label him with damning admiration. I have seen the picture of the boyish student in the long blue school uniform. He is leaning with a manly aura of bravado on a plinth, a score tucked under his arm, and his left hand in his pocket. He's talented and he wants to prove he's talented. He has polished his buttons. He's only nine years old when he enters the École, but he wants to begin composing. His composition teacher, M. Saint-Saëns who is, himself, only twenty-two years old, warns him about the "Mozart Factor" – the idea of becoming too much, too soon: the gluey, fallen soufflé that comes out of the oven before it is baked. He must avoid becoming the brat who places himself in the position of "dismissible." No one likes a genius. Prepare yourself, everyone tells him. The future will happen, but he will have to wait a lifetime because there are others in line ahead of him who are going to get their prizes first.

When people say *prepare yourself* to a young and precocious artist, they have two ulterior motives in mind. The first is that the establishment do not want the "young man in a hurry" to outshine those who have "paid their dues." That's a terrible artistic dictum – the horrible phrase, "paying your dues." There is no such thing as dues. One either learns the art and expresses what he has learned to the best of his ability or he's just trash. "Dues" is just another way to say, "Not so fast, buddy, there are people with more pressing claims." It means someone feels threatened by what is coming down the pike. It means that the artistic world is mean-spirited at heart and despises prodigies. That's what killed Mozart: the venom of other artists and his own prodigiousness.

The second thing that comes to mind is that the people who say *prepare yourself* have their own favourites they are betting on. They want their favourites to win. Art is a wager. They will do anything, even break the rules of a competition, to make sure their artist and no one else wins. There is no such thing as a competition under such circumstances. There is only the pre-chosen favourite and the *fait accompli*. Case closed.

I toss these thoughts around to pass the time as I wait, and consider that even when Fauré was ready to enter the École's competition in 1863, he won the competition but was disqualified as the winner on a technicality. The fix was in for him from the start. The École simply did not want another Mozart on their hands. They told their aspiring composer – not their best student, though, but the most aspiring one – that great music is made the same way great cognac is made: slowly.

Maybe the proverbial powers-that-be were putting their aspiring composer on notice for a reason. Every remark of encouragement, prizes included, is a double-edged sword. The mark of a stratified artistic milieu is the fear of original genius. That is what Gabriel Fauré was facing in 1863. He was a terrifying genius. The rules of the game, the laws of the milieu, say that a person should never tell a genius he is a genius until he is too old to care that he is.

A thin woman in a tweed skirt and a mohair cardigan, the very image of an archivist, appears at the desk and is motioned toward me by the old clerk, who senses her presence but does not look up from his copy of *Le Figaro*...he merely points a bony finger in my direction. She introduces herself in that clipped, rapid French that is so precise and over pronounced yet so hard to ascertain (the mark of a learned Parisian) that I do not catch her complete name and refer to her as Madame in my reply.

She leads the way, and I follow.

The box of papers I want to examine might give me a clue about how genius comes down to making brilliant ideas into brilliant realities. The book I am writing is about whether prizes and awards are indicators of genius. The archivist I am following up the grand staircase reminds me of a Modigliani figure. I feel as if I am back at school as I walk several paces behind her. I look over the railing into the atrium where students, mostly twenty-somethings, pore over scores, bite the tops off their biros, or scroll through their Facebook messages looking for clues as to who is saying what about whom, and who the social networks favour on that particular day. I explain to Madame that I am looking in the archives, letters, and correspondence for information about the Prix d'École of 1863.

The archivist stops abruptly. She turns and looks down on me two steps below her. I suspect I am about to be lectured, but instead she says nothing. She knows what I will find. I will discover boyish letters, supplications of consideration by Fauré for his entry, a feathery yet still uncertain hand in which notes flutter on the lines of a stave like birds on the metal balustrades of the Second Empire faux balcony outside my hotel window. Those birds stare in at me with the same penetrating look of *you aren't really serious, are you?* the archivist gives me with her silence.

We arrive at the top of the stairs. I look over my shoulder at the long flight I've just conquered. The prim, middle-aged woman is not even slightly breathless. She does the climb several times a day. I think she deserves a prize for being in such decent shape. She seats me at a teak table and I pull the chair under me as if I am about to embark on a multi-course meal. After disappearing behind the scenes, she returns with a grey box, which she places on the table, along with a pair of white cotton gloves.

I stare at the box. It is the reason I came to Paris. I wanted to see for myself what Gabriel Fauré experienced the first time he entered a competition and won, and lost, all for the same work.

Fauré entered the École Niedermeyer Composition Competition in 1863 at the age of seventeen with the idea that he had paid his dues during the years he had studied at the École, and that his score of Psalm 126, the "dream psalm," was the apotheosis of his learning.

Fauré should have won his first competition, but he didn't. The people in charge saw to it that he would not win. They may have had his best interests at heart, but that's just conjecture. He wasn't cognac. He was a kid who wanted to prove himself. He knew he was good. Maybe he was cocky, and the old guard spotted that and wanted to nip that in the bud. Instantaneous fame can be the worst thing that can happen to an artist.

I once heard a Canadian poet, Louis Dudek, remark that to be a poet at twenty is to be twenty, but to be a poet at forty is to be a poet. The bastard aspect in that piece of sage is that he said it to Leonard Cohen when Cohen was twenty. Put down? That's never been determined. *Ars longa, vita brevis*, as Chaucer said. A true artist must become a student of his art without any hope of graduating. Either way, success early or success late buries an artist. That's part of my thesis as well.

I put on the white gloves that could have been stolen from a street mime. The box contains the expected letters. The letter submitting the entry for the 1863 competition is polite, aulic, and addresses the judges of the École with due reverence. The next item in the box is the score. In Fauré's immature hand, the text of Psalm 126 is written out. It is the King James Version translated fairly precisely into French. It is an odd choice of psalm – a translation of a translation of a translation where all the levels of meaning compete with one another to convey their message. It reminds me of the cacophony I heard on the sidewalk as I approached the École.

The choice of Psalm 126 as the text for his score was, on Fauré's part, a cheeky venture. The psalm is about youthful hope, aspiration, the realization of dreams even when they seem impossible. It is a young man's psalm, and the choice of text suggests that perhaps Fauré knew that the fix was in, that no matter what he wrote he wouldn't win:

> When the Lord turned again the captivity of Zion, we were like them that dream. | Then was our mouth filled with laughter, and our tongue with singing: then said they among the heathen, The Lord hath done great things for them. | The Lord hath done great things for us; *whereof* we are glad. | Turn again our captivity, O Lord, as the streams in the south. | They that sow in tears shall reap in joy. | He that goeth forth weepeth, bearing precious seed, shall doubtless come again with rejoicing, and bring his sheaves *with him.*

The score for the psalm is melodic, pastoral, and lilting. It is beautiful not only for the music Fauré devises for it, but for the powerful sense of aspiration in the words. It is not a despondent psalm but a longing paean, and in the eyes of a young, aspiring composer who aches to achieve artistic excellence, he need only look at what the Lord had done for previous winners in terms of acclaim and advancement to realize that the same could be done for him.

The next item in the box is a copy of an anonymous letter from the chief judge of the competition, informing Fauré that his composition was by far the best and easily the winner, but the prize for the year would go to another student, Etienne Bernard, because Fauré had set Psalm 126 in the wrong key. The key should have been G, rather than D. The flabbergasted Fauré writes in response, rather hurriedly and in shaken handwriting – he could transpose the piece if it was the best submission. I can imagine the young man standing outside the director's office, his head bowed, and his voice choked as he pleads for an alteration in the opinion, but the judges' words are final. Perhaps that angry bang I heard coming from a keyboard earlier when I waited in the foyer was the ghost of the young, broken-hearted Gabriel Fauré, thwarted, frustrated, and aware that his best, *the* best, was not good enough.

I ask for the box of correspondence between Bernard and the judges from 1863. "Ah, oui," says the archivist. She knows I have put two and two together and am on to something. The score for Bernard's work was, indeed, in the proper key, but its text is mundane, to say the least. He chose Leviticus 23:36-39, a passage about what one should do on the sabbath to prepare a sacrifice to God, a meal of burnt offerings:

> These are the feasts of the Lord, which ye shall proclaim *to be*
> holy convocations, to offer an offering made by fire unto the
> Lord, a burnt offering, and a meat offering, a sacrifice,
> and drink offerings, every thing upon this day.

I shake my head. The gastronomically correct French would shudder to listen to such a litany of charred foods: yet for all its intense listing of rules, it follows the rules. Those who follow the rules of others rarely do anything original.

Orthodoxy in religion has its equal measure in art, and especially in literature and music. If someone in charge says, "This is the way it is going to be done," then everyone who is blessed in some measure follows the same rules. This is the *trieste* of art. Epigoni abound. Bernard was only doing his duty as a conscientious student composer in a brass-button coat when he chose his Levitican setting for choir and organ. But he wasn't making art. The passage has a kind of finger-wagging quality to it. It wasn't even material for a good restaurant review. I asked the archivist if a copy of his score was available in the École's holdings. After about twenty minutes, as she rustled around in the shelves behind the large teak door, she returned with a curt *non*.

While she was gone, I busied myself with Fauré's box of letters and records. I expected to find a letter where he expressed disappointment, perhaps even anger. There was a protest letter from Fauré's keyboard teacher, Camille Saint-Saëns, and a letter from a fellow student, Cesar Franck, asking for the judges to reconsider their decision, but they were politely worded and ineffectual. Someday, their voices would count as artillery in a debate about French music, but not in 1863. They were nobodies in those days. They were not part of the ruling clique. When artistic milieus are weak, or are going through a period of transition from old ways to the new, cliques always dominate the conversation. The old guard fights a rearguard action. They protect the old ways. Anger under such circumstances is futile. Cliques work best when they muffle any expressions of outrage.

I wanted to hear that note banged on the low keys in rage. That's what Lorca called *duende*, especially if it was a sour, minor chord. Instead, there was a polite reply by Fauré to the Director of the École stating that he would be trying again in the next competition, and he expressed his congratulations to M. Etienne Bernard. The handwriting, however, was emphatic. It was not the gentle, wispy strokes of the previous letters. Something had changed in Gabriel Fauré's character. He had ceased to be an innocent boy. He had become certain.

In the later life portraits of Fauré, his shock of white hair is the second thing one notices. The first thing is the upward tilt of his chin. Something happened to the shy and slightly awkward boy leaning on the plinth in the early photograph. Yes, he grew up; but growing up entails benchmarks, moments when someone is transformed by what they see or what they experience, moments from which there is no turning back. Such moments make the person who that individual becomes. Fauré became resolute in his mastery of a new idiom of musical composition that would become instantly recognizable to anyone in the world. He created the sound of French music.

In the box beneath the letter to the Director congratulating Bernard, I find Fauré's entry in the competition from the following year, 1864. The score is written in a bold, accurate hand. Every note makes a statement on the page, and to the ear every sound is there for a purpose, as if ennobled by the other notes around it. It is a composition that rises above itself. The opening bars of the piano and organ appear to be dissonant, working against each other. The organ presents a flowing repetition of melody, like a brook babbling through a forest – a steady, insistent presence that knows it will eventually build into a mighty river though it has only emerged as a spring from the earth.

I am being poetic about it, but the opening of the 1864 composition has always puzzled me. The male voices of the choir pick up the thread established by the piano and what they sing, oh, what they sing is magical. The literal translation of the opening lyrics, "Word equal with the Most High…" Equal. His word. God's word. The word given by divine inspiration. Fauré is laying down a statement. He is saying that on a level field, all things being equal, with no favourites, no predetermined scripts for the outcome of the competition, music alone will triumph. And when I examine the English lyrics, I see the composer reaching beyond himself as if to touch a distant star:

Word of God, one with the Most High,
In Whom alone we have our hope,
Eternal Day of heaven and earth,
We break the silence of the peaceful night;
Saviour Divine, cast your eyes upon us!

The words are the work of Jean Racine, a French poet and cleric who published *Hymnes traduites du Bréviaire romain* in 1688. For his key, Fauré found his métier, D-flat major, a key that years later his student, Maurice Ravel, would use for the famous *Concerto for the Left Hand*. I understand why Ravel chose that key as I examine the score for the 1864 competition. It is the key of suffering.

And therein resides the reason I sought out Fauré's composition and the story of its birth from a competition. Fauré is attempting to speak of eternal, divine love as if through a veil of human suffering. The second verse of Racine's breviary passage reads like a prayer for salvation from the fires and agonies of suffering:

> Pour on us the fire of your powerful grace,
> That all hell may flee at the sound of your voice;
> Banish the slumber of a weary soul,
> That brings forgetfulness of your laws!

Forgetfulness of rules and restrictions on art is more like it. Fauré realizes as he sets Racine's words to music that the earliest competitions were a form of agony. *Agon* is the ancient Greek word for competitor. Each autumn, the streets of Athens would run red with the blood of slaughtered animals as they passed through the city from the high summer pastures to the low grazing grounds where winter resources had to be carefully meted out. The strong would survive. The weak would have to be culled from the herds of sheep, and especially the goats. The slaughter of the goats, their bleating cries, their screams of agony, must have been horrible to the ear. *Tragedy.* Goat song. The key of tragedy is D-flat major. It is the key of man wrestling with his demons. It is the key in which Ravel set his *Concerto for the Left Hand* and gave it to the Austrian concert pianist Paul Wittgenstein, who had lost his right hand in the Great War. Ravel's choice of key is his homage to his teacher.

Fauré had stood up for his pupil against the same forces and doltish mentality that selected the work of Etienne Bernard. When Ravel was disqualified from a similar student competition thirty years later at the Paris Conservatoire, the key of D-flat major was Ravel's homage to his steadfast teacher, and a way of saying to Fauré, *I know what it is like to lose a competition with the best entry in the race, and I know the whole world has lost a competition of life versus death. The world has known* agony.

As I stare at the opening choral passages of Fauré's entry for the 1864 competition, I can hear in my head the low male voices of the chorus. They're like souls of the damned crying out from the depths of Dante's hell. I know where I had heard them recently. The voices were the ones I'd heard crying from a frame on a gallery wall.

A few days ago, when I was visiting the D'Orsay, I came across a small exhibition of etchings by the early twentieth-century artist, Andre Devaumbez. As I paused in front of one of Devaumbez's works, Fauré's composition jumped into my head, and I began to weep. Devaumbez, Ravel, and so many others whose works vanished into the muds at Verdun – they understood what suffering was.

The etching by Devaumbez that I could not pass by – I spent two hours studying it intensely – is of a group of soldiers, observed from a high vantage point. In the centre of the etching is a black dot. It is a priest. The jagged outlines around the black dot are the troops taking Mass and receiving the Last Rites before they march out into the white void of no man's land. Ravel served in the French artillery, and the experience drove him to deafness, so that for the remainder of his life he clung to the memory of music rather than its reality, just as Beethoven had done a century earlier. And as I stood and stared at those figures, those men clustered around the black dot, searching for an inner solace and peace that offered them only fear and uncertainty, I heard the male voices that emerge from the dissonance of the opening of Fauré's 1864 composition: "We break the silence of the peaceful night...cast your eyes upon us!" Their voices are trapped in the key of mourning, and only prayer offers them a way out.

But the key of D-flat major has another meaning. It is not merely the key of suffering and despair, but of emergence, of the individual rising out of the depths of despair and defeat and finding the human soul intact, the small light that still shines after a long darkness. It is the key that says a composer has come to an epiphany, has seen something divine beyond our suffering, and something greater than ourselves rising out of our despair, and is willing to champion that small spark and set it ablaze amidst the agony and tragedy, to offer a promise of redemption. Fauré's 1864 composition, *Cantique de Jean Racine,* concludes with the lyrics:

O Christ, look with favour upon your faithful people
Now gathered here to praise you;
Receive their hymns offered to your immortal glory;
May they go forth filled with your gifts.

And with that, Fauré *was* filled with something miraculous. There was no question. To deny him the prize in the 1864 competition would have been a travesty against art. The *Cantique de Jean Racine* won the Prix d'École Niedermeyer that year. The last item in the box is Fauré's thank-you letter to the Director of the École. And as I tuck it away with the other papers I have spent the morning reading, I ask myself how many people may have heard of the Prix d'École Niedermeyer as opposed to how many who have heard the *Cantique de Jean Racine.* The prize meant nothing; the work of art it generated has delivered its message of redemption to millions. Even if it had not won, I am convinced the *Cantique* would, to this day, still possess the power to move those who hear it to tears of hope and awe.

I cannot forget the first time I heard the *Cantique*. I was a student and had just missed out on a scholarship at the university. I had better marks, an elderly professor told me, but there was another student, the student who won, who they said was more deserving. "These things are all political," I was told. I sorely wanted that scholarship; it would have assured me a place in graduate school the next year. The other student, the one who got the prize, got the spot at grad school and promptly failed out.

The sad aspect of competitions is that one always wonders afterwards what might have been. What would have happened to *Finnegan's Wake* if *Ulysses* had established Joyce's reputation to the degree where he and not Pearl S. Buck won the Nobel. Reason dictates that prizes do not mean anything. They are indicators of the moment when preference, choice, politics, unseen circumstances, favouritism, artistic stupidity, and even bad luck play into the process of deciding the outcome of agonized competitors.

Hearing the *Cantique de Jean Racine* at a concert the night I received the news about the scholarship changed me and the way I look at the world. I had never heard a piece of music so beautiful. Then I learned of the story of its birth and I came to believe – yes, believe – what the philosopher Boethius argued in his *Consolation of Philosophy*, namely that all fame is rumour, that what is real lasts, and what is too distant to see is never far away from us, and what is painful is true. Boethius calls it heaven. And to hear Fauré's *Cantique* is to acquire some inkling of what heaven might be like for those who choose to believe it exists.

Ars longa, vita brevis.

One hundred and fifty years after it was composed, I hold in my hand the original score for the *Cantique de Jean Racine*, and the music is even more beautiful today because it has endured the test of time. I return the box to the archivist's desk. She must have gone for lunch because I cannot find her when I peer through the tall teak door. I decide it is also time I lunched.

As I reach the bottom step on the grand staircase, I catch sight of an old friend crossing the mezzanine. Paul Rouger is conductor of Les Solistes Français, a brilliant ensemble that performs frequently during the summer months in Sainte-Chapelle. In the embrace of the soaring medieval stained glass, Rouger's treatment of classics such as Vivaldi's *Four Seasons* and Vitali's *Chaconne for Violin* create a reverence in the moment that has moved me to trembling more than once.

I got to know Paul the summer my daughter was ten and I brought her to Paris. We had front row seats. During Fauré's *Nocturne,* one of the horsehairs on Paul's bow came loose and without missing a beat, he plucked it and tossed it to the stage. When the concert finished, my daughter ran up and grabbed the strand as a souvenir. When he asked her what she thought of the concert, she replied, "I thought I was in heaven." That is how our friendship began.

We pause for a moment. I don't want to keep him. He says he has to get across town for a rehearsal for a concert that evening. I ask him what the group will be playing.

"Fauré's *Cantique de Jean Racine,*" he said.

You are justified in thinking that this is a convenient moment of *deus ex machina,* but it is not. He really is performing the *Cantique* with Les Solistes and the Choir of Saint-Sulpice. There are moments in one's life of tremendous serendipity and this is one of them. He rummages in his pocket and holds out two tickets. "Just one," I say. "I'm on research here alone. I've been researching the *Cantique.*" He smiles, pats me on the shoulder. "Let's talk about it after this evening's concert. *À bientôt.*"

Entering Sainte-Chapelle is an experience akin to dying and being reborn. Through the courtyard of the Palais de Justice, one enters a dark, tomb-like portal. Over the door is a medieval frieze of Christ releasing the souls of the righteous from the jaws of Hell. They are the virtuous ones, *born sub Julio,* as Dante describes it, who wait in Hell for the coming of Christ and a redemption they anticipate will happen someday. I wonder if that was how Gabriel Fauré felt when he received news that his setting of Psalm 126 was denied the prize. Waiting and longing, uncertain if redemption will ever come, staying strong, patient, and believing, he picks up his pen. He hears the low voices intoning. He finds the notes that explain the human heart. Patience is the hardest part of life for an artist who is certain of his art.

It is 7 p.m. on a June evening as I take my seat in the front row, just down from where my daughter and I sat a decade before. Sainte-Chapelle always brings me to the verge of wordlessness. It was built by Louis IX of France to house the Crown of Thorns. The word *agony* runs through my mind. The darkness of agony… and then transcendent beauty. I am part of a moment and place, and I am in that moment of convergence when two works of art meet and time stands still. The choir files in, followed by Les Solistes, and then Rouger. The orchestra tunes, the singers clear their throats and come to attention. The audience falls silent. The light of the solstice sun beams through the north wall on which the prophets and the singers of psalms are depicted in the fire of ancient glass. And as I look up at the jewel-toned image of David playing his harp, the brilliance begins to sing.

Martha Bátiz

SUSPENDED

"You cannot stay there forever," Ben says, trying to muffle his desperation.

Ben is losing his patience. He looks so much like Jason. Or Jason like him. Same pointy nose and ears, almost like an elf's; the same blue eyes. I touch the wall. *Blue Lagoon 2054-40* – a colour I chose not because of its corny name recalling illicit memories of puberty, but after hours of visits to the hardware store and the comparing of samples. I wanted to sleep engulfed by the balminess of those eyes. I wanted for that blue to watch me, touch me, to be with me. I close my hand into a fist and hit the wall. It hurts. I scratch at the paint with my fingernails, struggling to reveal the white drywall. My index finger bleeds a little and I enjoy it. I want to peel off the paint; peel off my skin.

Ben breathes through his teeth, loudly, like a bull, and leaves. I am relieved and as I peel tiny lagoons of paint off the wall, I remember Jason talking about crabs. How they outgrow their shells and shed them.

"It's called moulting," he said, and I wish I had videotaped him saying that so I could hear his eight-year-old voice again. Moulting. It can take months, sometimes. How long will it take me to peel the paint off the entire bedroom? Will I ever moult out of this pain?

He was right: I cannot stay in bed forever. I must use the washroom. A stranger gazes back at me when I look in the mirror. My eyebrows have gone grey, yet I got my period this morning. What a joke, I think, to have my body remind me at this precise moment that I am empty inside. I inspect my greasy hair, my swollen eyes. The few hairs that grow on my chin have decided not to match my eyebrows and are still black and coarse. I wish my entire body were covered in hair, like thorns. Perhaps it would make me stronger.

The red stains in my underwear take me to the days when I used to lie back on medical tables, feet in the stirrups, my body a war zone where injections, blood letting, ultrasounds, medications, prayers, and sperm failed to create the miracle of life. Ben masturbating in the room next door, looking at naked women (and men?) who were nothing like us, while I lay open-legged in front of yet another doctor who promised us success. And then, when we were about to give up, a faint hormone count, a *linea nigra* writing a promise from my pubic bone to my belly button, my breasts full of hope and milk and Jason, finally, after nine long months, in my arms. I suppress the urge to open the photo albums and peruse our pictures. I know my favourites by heart: the one where Ben is hugging me from behind, cradling my pregnant stomach; the one where we're together, crying with joy, holding our newborn; the one where you can clearly tell, for the first time, that Jason will have his father's deep blue eyes.

My arms hurt. Their emptiness hurts. So do the bruises. I've been wearing long sleeves so Ben doesn't notice that I've been pinching my arms, pinching them out of hatred, because there is now nothing for them to hold.

I go back to bed and look up at the ceiling. I regret having paid extra for it to have a smooth finish. A textured ceiling would be more interesting to look at. The room at my mother's house when I was growing up had what is called a popcorn finish. I can picture it perfectly because, after my first boyfriend broke up with me, I spent three weeks in bed, crying, listening to old Edith Piaf records, wondering what had gone wrong and how would I manage to continue living. Everything hurts so much when you're sixteen. Everything seems so hopeless. I remember driving at full speed thinking I wanted to crash. I remember wanting to walk into traffic at a busy intersection. What stopped me? And why didn't it stop him?

"How was school?" I asked, serving Jason a spoonful of mashed potatoes, his favourite.

"Fine, but I'm not hungry," he replied, leaving the plate untouched.

I should have known something was wrong. I should have insisted that he eat. But I had been sixteen once and self-conscious about my weight so I tried to be understanding. He was a straight-A student, popular among his friends. Why worry? Ben was happy to eat whatever our son didn't want – "Dad is like that little dinosaur under the Flintstones' kitchen sink that eats everything," Jason used to say – so I let it be. Then he stopped showering. He started skipping classes. His grades dropped.

"Where were you? The principal called!" I'd scolded him. But instead of answering, he'd rushed up to his bedroom and slammed the door behind him. Why hadn't I run after him to demand answers? I did, once, and he pushed me so hard I almost fell down the stairs. We didn't tell Ben. Jason apologized, looked genuinely scared. We were both afraid.

I clench my teeth at the memory. My eyes well up, and by the time Ben comes into the room I am curled up in a corner of the bed.

"Let's give you a shower, come on," he says, gently. I curl up ever tighter, pretending to be a millipede. Jason would have been able to read my body. He was the one who taught me about millipedes to begin with. I want to be one, but Ben won't let me. He pulls the bed sheets away and I let out a cry.

"You smell bad. I'll get the bed clean for you," he says, his blue eyes fixed on mine. Only then do I notice his hair has gone grey, too. He reminds me of his father. He's holding the stained blanket in his hand. "I need to wash this."

I bring my nose to my armpit, then lift the T-shirt to my nose and inhale. A knot curls up in my throat.

"It doesn't smell like him anymore, Ben!"

He drops the blanket and sits beside me, possibly trying to decide whether to hug me or not. I cry harder.

"I'll bring you another shirt from his drawer," he says.

But I don't want that. I want one from his laundry hamper. I want one that smells like him. Like his teenage deodorant and cologne and sweat. Only his dirty clothes hold traces of his life. I want to wear him.

Ben holds up a tissue for me and I blow my nose. I dry my eyes; he leads me to the washroom and starts running the shower. I let him undress me, forgetting about the bruises on my arms.

"What have you been doing to yourself?" he asks, looking at me with pity and concern. I don't know how to answer, so I hug the shirt I've been wearing for days until the water is warm enough for me to get in. He applies shampoo to my hair, washes my body with soap.

I remember how I washed Jason's body when he was little. It was always a struggle to get him into the water because he'd rather keep playing with his toys or watching TV.

"Jason! Bath time!" I would call from upstairs.

His usual reply of "Not yet!" was almost a ritual, repeating itself until I lost my patience and went downstairs to fetch him, to chase him up the stairs.

"I'm a T-Rex and I'm going to get you!" I roared.

Jason would laugh and correct me: "You're more like a *Diplodocus*, Mom! Good try!"

I'd pretend to get angry and we'd both go upstairs, laughing. Then he would get in the water and enjoy the touch of my hand as I rubbed his back and lathered his head. I loved the aroma of his freshly washed hair, the lotion I applied on his body. I make a mental note to buy more so I can inhale and think of him.

The silence between me and Ben brings me back to the present. I wonder what he's thinking about. I know not to ask because he always gives me the strangest answers, like that one time after dinner, when I asked him what he was thinking about and he said, "The Romans." Who thinks about the Romans? I'm about to ask if he remembers how much Jason enjoyed the loofah when he tells me to take my time rinsing while he changes the bed sheets. He leaves before I can ask any questions. I panic – what bed sheets? Jason's? But I need those. I'll sleep better if I can curl up against the shape of his body. I rush out of the shower to tell Ben I want to sleep in Jason's room, but I slip and fall, making everything wet around me.

"Where are you going?" Ben asks, exasperated. "Why couldn't you wait?"

"The bed sheets! I want Jason's bed sheets…" I mumble, ashamed.

Ben looks at me; annoyed, concerned.

"The ones that were on his bed?"

I nod.

"Don't you remember?"

I shake my head. Remember what?

"You buried him in them. You wanted his coffin to have his bed sheets and his blanket. You wanted him to—"

I feel my eyes opening wide.

"To be more comfortable," I say, my voice cracking at the memory of his empty bed, and of my asking the lady at the funeral home to make sure to cover him to keep him warm. *My son never liked the cold. He was scared of the dark.*

"Come on, get up. Are you hurt?" Ben helps me to my feet. "Careful with the puddle on the floor," he adds, as if water could hurt me, as if there was anything else in the world that could hurt me.

I am back in bed, looking at the dismal ceiling. I wish it were a movie screen where I could play our happiest moments with Jason. His first birthday. The unexpected instant he touched the sand at the beach and raised his feet up saying, "Ew! Gross!" The moment he learned to ride a bike. When he bit into a hot dog and lost his first tooth. All those times he talked about spiders and crocodiles. The nights he came to our bed, right here, and cuddled up between us, hiding from nightmares. He came to us trying to feel safe, but I was the one who was comforted by his little foot beside me, the smell of strawberry toothpaste on his breath, the soft rhythm of his beating heart.

I remember all of these things. The morning routine: get up, get dressed, have breakfast, make lunch, kiss goodbye, go to school, go to work, come back from work and school, have dinner together, talk about our days, do homework, take a shower, read a story, go to sleep. Repeat. If only life were a video where you could hit the repeat button. I would press that button endlessly, to experience that precious routine again and again.

I lift the T-shirt to my nose and inhale. Yes, it smells like him. Only it's the him that wouldn't talk anymore. The him who didn't want to share any details about his life with me. The him who wasn't him anymore. Ben said it would pass. It was a phase.

"He's a teenager," he said.

Ben walks into the room carrying a tray of food and I'm suddenly furious because it wasn't a phase, and it didn't pass. And how was "he's a teenager" supposed to be of any help? At the moment he's close enough, I knock the tray up in the air and cry, "I hate you, I hate you, I hate you!" until my yelling becomes sobbing and then nothing because I'm drowning in my voice and my tears.

I'm alone in the room and there are broken plates on the floor, and food all over the clean bed sheets. I realize the soup was hot and my skin is burning, my leg is blistering, but I don't care because my shirt no longer smells like him but like tomato sauce, and the red stain will never wash away, yet his smell will.

I wish I were a praying mantis, but I remember Jason was afraid of them because the mommies eat the daddies, and I hate Ben even more.

The church was full; it was standing room only. Jason hated going to church and I told Ben we should have the service elsewhere, but he wouldn't hear of it. I don't remember what was said; what passages of the Bible were read. I don't recall who was there, only that many young people came over to me with stories I had never heard, stories about hilarious things that Jason had done. Young people I had never met but who said they were close friends of his. I tried to listen but it was too much, too much. The church was full and some people weren't wearing black. I felt like telling them off – how dare you show up not wearing black, don't you know my son is dead? But I wasn't strong enough. Ben had to hold me by the arm, and it took a huge effort for me to stay composed. I had just kissed my dead son's cheeks. He was cold – it took me by surprise and I shivered. Stupid! What was I expecting? That coldness was all I could think about when Mass began. My entire attention was focused on my lips and the indelible memory they now held. I wanted to scream. There is my son, I thought, staring at the casket. He will remain there forever. His body will swell and decompose in that box. My beautiful son's eyes will be pushed out of their sockets, his inner organs will explode and his rosy skin will turn black before he's reduced to mere bones. He was once an unborn child kicking vigorously inside my womb. It had been a miracle to feel such movement. But now, nothing. Soon to be dust. Unmoving dust.

Ben comes in, mop and bucket in hand, to clean up my mess. I'm ashamed of myself and get out of bed to help. My leg hurts because of the burn, but I say nothing. Together, we pick up pieces of ceramic and bits of food, in silence. I help him change the bed sheets and reluctantly agree to change into another one of Jason's shirts.

"Thank you for helping," Ben says, his blue lagoon eyes fixed on mine. They have lost their spark but they are still beautiful. Jason's eyes. I stare at Ben, trying to find my son.

"Do you know where Jason is?" I asked Ben over the phone, flustered, in a hurry, on the way to my car. "They called from school. He didn't show up again, they're worried. I've been calling him on his cell phone and at home but there's no answer."

"Again? Tell him he's really in trouble this time!" Ben blurted out.

I hung up. I had to find him. I drove too fast; running red lights and coasting through stop signs, trying to get back to the house as soon as possible. This time something was wrong. Everything felt wrong.

When I got home, I ran up the stairs to his room, searching my mind for the right words to say. I wanted to see him. Now I can't un-see him, un-find him, un-live my scream, my attempt to revive him only to discover how heavy he was, how open his eyes were, so open and blue and lifeless, like a picture of the lake. Then there was the empty pill container – where did he get that? The ambulance, the police car; Ben's face, his eyes a tempestuous ocean. He hugged me but I hit him, I hit him on the chest, yelling, "I told you! I told you!"

"Mommy, what do you think I should be when I grow up?" Jason asked once, when we were in the car. I looked in the rear-view mirror and found his face.

"I don't know. Whatever makes you happy."

He looked very serious and I took advantage of us being stopped at a red light to admire his face. He was growing so fast! Almost ten in a couple of months.

"I think I want to be a mathematician, like Daddy, and an administrator like you, but also a scientist who works with insects and dinosaurs."

I laughed.

"That sounds perfect, my love."

It was supposed to be perfect. He was supposed to graduate high school, go to university, get married, find a job, live a happy life. I was supposed to watch him do all that. And now there is nothing. We have nothing. We are nothing. This cannot be possible, this is a nightmare. This is not real.

"Ben!" I cry out.

I hear his steps coming up the stairs two by two. I'm sorry I scared him.

"The note! Bring me the note!"

He stands at the door of the bedroom.

"Why do you want it now?"

I shake my head.

"I forget what he said. I want to read it again. I don't remember his writing. I want to touch the last thing that he touched."

Ben walks out to the hallway and returns a few moments later. He sits next to me and hands me a folded piece of paper.

It's the original, not the photocopy the police left us when our home was considered a crime scene. His room, a crime scene. I shake my head to banish that unbelievable phrase from my mind.

My eyes are brewing another storm. I have trouble unfolding the letter. Ben is silent beside me, his blue eyes fixed on the wall that looks like it has some kind of smallpox. Everything around us is ailing.

I lift the paper into the light – my gaze, my breath suspended.

Andrea Bradley

NO ONE IS
WATCHING

Number 16 sat tucked into the elbow of our street like a forgotten child. It was a faded, mute bungalow, nearly swallowed up by the grass. It hadn't changed in the month since we'd moved in. I'd almost stopped looking at it, but today, something caught my eye. A door, a window – something, round the side of the house, swinging shut as we drove by.

"Does someone live there now?" I asked.

Laura, my wife, was in the passenger seat, a phone on each knee. She thumbed distractedly through work emails. She was always like this when she had a flight to catch, like part of her was already gone.

"Where?" she asked.

"Number 16."

"Not that I know of," she said.

"I thought I saw something. An animal," I said.

"Lots of those around," she muttered, her eyebrows knit together with whatever urgent request was coming to her from Toronto.

That evening, I curled into the corner of the couch, the TV volume turned down low so I could hear if Abel called. I always hated the first night of Laura being away. After a day or two, I settled into a solitary pattern, but the first night every sense would be on alert, filtering through sounds that cannot be her, listening for small feet on stairs, knocks at the door, the clicking and creaking and banging of a house that's seen too many winters. Even the glow of the TV is unsettling during those first nights alone.

I gave up on the movie an hour in. As I climbed the stairs, I heard a whimper from Abel's room. I went to him, put my hand to his head, smoothed his dark hair until his breath evened. Outside, the moon shone wanly, but stronger than the weak glow of the single lamp on our street. I moved to the window and looked at the houses shuttered among the trees. A few doors down, a TV flickered behind half-closed drapes. Number 16 sat beyond that, a darker patch in the dark. I stared that way until my eyes blurred, until I saw – until I thought I saw – something move. Crouch-backed and tentative, like a raccoon. I blinked. Whatever it was had darted back into the trees.

I pulled the window shut, locked it, and closed the blinds. I looked at Abel and told my heart to slow, for him, then I climbed into his bed and curled around him and counted each exhale until I slept.

When Laura is here, she is my partner. I am one type of mom and she is one type of mom and we are firm and sorted, like shapes. When Laura is away, I become unfixed. I retreat into and out of myself, all at once, becoming too aware of the world around me and fixating on my own shortcomings.

So, walking Abel to school, I was thinking of Laura and the eyes on the street and what all our small-town neighbours made of our half-here, half-there relationship. I waved at Judy, the grey-haired lady at number 20, her face fossilized from twenty years of hard smoking. She waved back, fingers wiggling at Abel. I squeezed his shoulder, wanting him to smile brightly for her benefit, but that's not his style.

"Can we pretend to be something?" He turned his face up at me.

"Sure, like what?" I asked.

"Let's be airplanes." Abel spread his wings wide and ran ahead. I jogged after him, but slowed as we got to number 16. I walked to the edge of the lawn. The grass hissed softly in the breeze. A piece of blue fabric lay in the ditch – a shirt maybe – matted by mud and rain, planed like the curve of a shoulder blade. There were cracks between the boards that covered the windows. I imagined the inside, dust motes hanging suspended in the shafts of light. I imagined walking through the empty rooms. I imagined footsteps behind me, soft and curious.

A screen door hung open at the side of the house. Had it always?

"Mom." Abel's voice came from my elbow. "What are you doing?"

I imagined Abel, alone, in a boarded-up house, terror pinning him to the floor. I swallowed hard.

"Come on, let's get you to school," I said. I turned from number 16, throwing reason and logic up to shield my back. *No one is watching. There is no one inside.*

A cry woke me. I thought of Abel first and sat up in bed. The shapes in my room were grainy and distorted in the dark. I breathed quietly, straining to hear. The fridge hummed downstairs. Something clicked in the bathroom. Outside, insects chirped.

The cry came again, and this time I figured out where it was coming from. Abel's room. I ran in and found him curled in the corner of his bed, face to the wall. I watched his back for a few seconds, moving in and out. In my mind, I touched his shoulder. In my mind, he turned, his face empty, gone, a ghoulish mask.

Stop it. Stop making things up. You're the adult.

I touched Abel's forehead with the tips of my fingers. His eyes flittered as he dreamed. I looked out his window and stared down at our street. There were no house lights on that night, no comforting flicker of late night TV. There was only the one streetlight, the puddled glow beneath it and, in that light, a girl.

She was Abel's size, but I couldn't tell her age. Her head was turned away. One second, I thought she was a child, the next she seemed older. Her hair, white-blond and tangled, hung down her back. Her clothes were several sizes too big: a pale, scuffed sweater, wrinkled tights, no shoes.

My heart felt torn in two. One side urged me to run downstairs and gather her in. But something else rooted me to the floor. To see. To wait and see.

The girl was bent over to one side and she began to limp in a slow circle. She turned toward me, hair a curtain across her face. My fingers on the blinds felt like wood, clumsy. Not mine. I stared until the night blotted my vision. She lifted her head and I swear she saw me, though her eyes were hollowed black.

I dropped the blinds, bit hard on my lip.

You are an adult. Ghosts aren't real. Out there is a person who needs your help.

When I lifted the blinds, she was gone.

"You called me eleven times and you didn't call the cops?"

In the day, night terror scrubbed away, I realized what I looked like to Laura – desperate for her attention, crazy.

"You weren't there," I said, which was the pin I pushed in every argument, though it filled me with self-loathing and regret.

Laura ran her fingers through her short brown hair, spiking it in all directions. Even on the tiny horizontal screen of my phone, I could tell she was tired. She looked down, distracted for a moment, probably checking her work phone. Then she looked back at me.

"Here's what you're going to do. Call the police. Not 911, the non-urgent line. Tell them what you heard and saw. Explain that you're alone with a kid and didn't feel safe going out at night. Tell them you weren't thinking straight in the middle of the night but it's bugging you now. Okay?"

I nodded, gripping my coffee.

"Are you going to be alright?"

I nodded again. I didn't trust myself to speak. Bitter words beat themselves against my lips, like trapped moths.

"It's just a few more days. I'll call you during the lunch recess. Is Abel okay?"

"He's still sleeping," I said.

"Give him a kiss for me when he wakes up. I've got to go. I'm cross-examining today." Laura looked at me worried, appraising. "I love you," she said.

I picked my way along the matted path. Laura and Abel were sleeping at home, but I had found myself waking early, every day since that night. It had been a week ago, and nothing had changed.

The cops had taken my statement. They were young and bored with being small-town Ontario cops.

"And was anyone else home when you saw the girl outside?"

"Just Abel, my son. He was sleeping," I'd said.

"Where was your husband, ma'am?"

"My *wife* was in Toronto, for work. She's a lawyer."

I'd watched them carefully for a reaction, but they gave me nothing. Not the slightest raise of an eyebrow. I don't know what I was expecting. We've all been trained not to react to other people's stories and they're professional non-reactors.

I looked down at my running shoes, the tips turning dark with dew. In the morning, the woods were saturated with water and alive with the furtive, secret sounds of prey. In the morning,

I thought best. I ran through the reasons that brought us north, the things that were pulling us apart, and the things that held us together. Laura was home for a few days only and I should've made the most of it, but instead I was there. I chose to be alone.

The cops did nothing about the girl. I saw them walk down the street, knocking on doors. Not too many people live on our street and most are over 60, maybe hard of hearing, maybe used to not hearing. I saw a few of them stand on their porch, shake their heads. The cops stopped at number 16. I saw them disappear around the side of the house, then come back around shortly after. I don't know if they went inside.

Something moved in the undergrowth, off to my right. I paused, my heart pacing a beat faster. I peered into the woods. Something was moving the raspberry bushes, pushing them to sway out of tempo with the wind. I closed a fist around the keys in my pocket, imagined something lunging out at me, driving the jagged metal into skin at its neck. Rubbery, resistant. A struggle against snarling, snapping jaws. A rabid raccoon. A feral child.

A grouse stepped out from the bush, its tiny head twitching. I relaxed my grip on my keys, slowed my breathing, and watched until it disappeared again.

I was starting to wonder if I had seen the girl. Maybe it was some kind of waking dream. A night terror. My mother told me I'd had them as a child, but it was nothing I could remember. I picked up speed along the trail, stretching out my legs until I could feel it in my hips. Suddenly, I wanted to get home, quickly. I wanted to climb into our still-warm bed and watch Laura sleep. She looked so different, sleeping, all the grey worry of the life we've built smoothed away. I breathed in the pine scent. I was so deep inside my thoughts that I stopped noticing what was around me. My path took me almost to the back of the house before I realized where I was.

From the back, the house was just as decrepit. There were windows on this side, too, boarded up, just like the front. There was a grey fence, half prone, separating the backyard from the path that ran through the woods behind our street. Somehow, I had never explored this way. I'd spent many mornings in the woods, but I'd chosen my routes, and didn't stray close to the backyards. I'd left the city so I didn't have to always be looking at other people's business.

My heart hammered. I hesitated for a minute, my muscles coiled, before I knew I had to. I picked my way over the broken fence and into the tall grass. I felt like I had stepped through glass, like I had crossed some unspoken boundary between reality and the unreality that was the girl. A pile of junk stood in one corner of the yard. A blue plastic barrel, cracked at the top. A rusted old stepladder lying on its side. A wooden box, one that might hold toys or tools, its top smashed in. There was a swing set on the other side of the yard. Chains hung down from the bar, the plastic seat fallen to the ground below. I swallowed hard.

I walked to the house, to the boarded-up windows. I pressed my fingers to the boards. The wood was cool and rough. I peered between the slats and caught my breath.

The room was not empty. Far from it. I was looking into the kitchen. The fridge stood open on one side. There was a stove, piled with tattered grass and insulation. There were yellowed newspapers on the floor, a broken table, scattered chairs. Beyond a doorway, I could make out more disorder in the dim rooms beyond. A stack of mattresses on a sagging floor, broken bottles, spray-painted walls. There was so much clutter, it would be easy for someone to hide. My heart stood still while I stared. I waited for something to cross my vision, for a shadow to flicker.

Nothing moved.

I backed away from number 16 so that eyes could not crawl on my back. I went around the side of the house, as the morning woods no longer seemed a place of life. I did not breathe until I was on our street again, the spell broken.

"Why does it have to be you? Can't one of the other partners fill in?"

Laura stared back at me with guarded eyes. Our dinners sat, barely touched, in front of us. We'd waited to eat until Abel went to bed, so that we could have this time together. So we could argue in peace.

"You know I can't pass it off, Char. This is my file. I've been working on it for two years. When we moved here, this was part of the deal. I need to work."

"Yeah, I know," I said. I had nothing to throw back at her, really. I don't know what I thought would happen when we came up here. I knew she would be gone much of the time. I just thought that our time together would mean more. There would be no distractions when she was here. I thought she would slowly, gradually, come around to the quiet. She would be forced to take on less work, to find something else to do.

"Why don't you and Abel come with me? You haven't even seen the apartment yet."

"And Abel would just miss school?"

"Just for a few days," Laura said. She was trying. I knew she was trying.

"What's the point? It's not like we'll see you any more than we do now."

Laura shook her head. She couldn't argue with that. The next day, I'd drive her to the airport and it would be Abel and me, alone again.

I walked Abel to school the next day, after bringing Laura to her 6 a.m. flight. Abel held my hand at first and it made my throat catch, how much he needed me sometimes. By the time we got to number 16, he'd let go and was walking ten paces behind me. I stopped to wait. In the sunshine, the house just looked tired.

"Why do you keep looking at it?" Abel asked. I reached for his hand again, but he was fiddling with the straps of his backpack.

"I'm just waiting for you," I said.

"It's rude to stare."

"Not at a house," I said, half-smiling.

"At the people who live there," Abel said. He was looking down, so he couldn't see the expression on my face. I smoothed my features into neutrality.

"No one lives there," I said carefully.

"*Someone* does," he said.

"Who? Have you seen them?" I felt I needed to tread carefully. Ask the wrong question and Abel will lose interest. Ask the wrong question, and he'll start making things up.

"Yeah."

"Do any kids live there? Do they go to your school?"

Abel shook his head.

"But you've seen them?" I pressed.

Abel nodded. "She doesn't play."

Cold swept over me.

"What do you mean?"

"She just can't," Abel shrugged, his mind already turning to other things. He held his backpack over his head and turned to see his shadow, the holes of the straps making big eyes.

"Let's pretend to be monsters," he said.

I didn't call the cops again. What was I going to tell them? Abel's just a kid. He makes up stories all the time. I told them about the girl the first time. I told them. They should have done their job.

Another cry broke the night. I pushed my feet to the floor, the cold air wrapping my shins. I walked quickly to the window, lifted the blinds. The backyard was a wall of black. Out there, the trees run all the way to the highway. When the sound came again, I knew what it was.

A siren. Just a siren, on the highway out back. I went to the bed and lay down, my body stiff. Laura's side of the bed was untouched. I placed my hand on the smooth sheets, imagined her hand covering mine.

The sound of the siren faded and I closed my eyes. I wondered what she was doing that night, whether she was alone in our apartment, eating takeout and highlighting her notes, or out with one of the other partners, martinis and complaints about their wives.

I would do better by her. I would try harder. For Abel.

The siren's wailing grew again and this time it came from the front of the house. I tried to ignore it, but it rose and rose until it seemed to come from our front lawn. I padded to Abel's room and saw the walls shimmering with colour. Abel turned in bed, called softly, and fell back into that miraculous sleep of childhood.

I opened the blinds and looked out onto our street. Cedar Crescent was alive with light and sound. Two police cars and an ambulance had parked near the bend, in front of number 16. I watched as the lights in neighbouring houses flickered on. I watched as grey-haired, robed figures stumbled out into the night. I watched Judy's cigarette flickering red, as she stood talking to two officers beside their cruiser. I watched as the stretcher appeared from around the other side of number 16, and even from the window, I could see that the sheet was stretched from end to end.

The lump in the middle was tiny.

It was barely there.

Priscila Uppal

ELEVATOR SHOES

Ten years ago my cousin Diana was in an elevator accident. Yes, apparently the fear that ripples across your consciousness when an elevator jars against the floor beams or stops slightly short and jams or simply ascends at a breakneck pace through dozens of indifferent numbers is real. That fear: what if the elevator cables snap and all of a sudden the elevator shuttles uncontrollably down to the ground?

We tell ourselves these things never happen. Urban myths. Miniature horror stories designed to keep bratty kids in line. But they do happen. Every day. We just tell ourselves they don't so we can go to the office or visit a friend's new one-bedroom condo on the lakeshore or book an appointment at the chiropractor to take care of that annoying neck spasm that doesn't seem to be going away even after several microwaved Magic Bags, muscle rubs and YouTube neck exercises.

That's where my cousin Diana was headed – the chiropractor. To the third floor of a twelve-storey building.

She could have taken the stairs, but most people don't, and let me venture to say most Brazilian women don't. Because of their high-heeled shoes. Oh, they can walk across the treacherous cobblestone streets of Copacabana like it's a runway catwalk for miles and miles and never break a sweat or wince. Brazilian women can suffer shoes for the sake of beauty – or should I say dignity – yes, for the sake of dignity – for life is very difficult and what else do we have but the illusion of floating through it on golden heels or

144

red straps – Brazilian women can suffer shoes and all manner of indignities like no one else.

Diana had been suffering the indignity of taking care of her bi-polar suicidal sister for the past three months. I say indignity because her sister, Isabel, could help herself but won't. She has a psychiatrist she refuses to see and medication she refuses to take and she even has a very expensive law degree she refuses to use. So whenever Isabel attempts to kill herself – which is about every six months or so – the staff at the Emergency Psychiatric Ward joke that Isabel ought to pay rent and have her own sui-cidal express taxi service – Diana is forced to take time off her job at the audio equipment distributor office where she answers phones and inputs order forms for microphones and speakers and turntables and recording equipment for everything from bat mizvah gifts to bar karaoke nights to some seriously famous clients who outfit their own hip hop studios. One night, she met someone so famous – I can't tell you who because she signed a confidentiality agreement – that even his breath, she said, smelled of $$$. And he'd flirted with her a little – compliment-ing her on her Rainbow Open-Toed Ankle-Strapped Studded Accent High Heels. "Those are I-know-who-I-am shoes," he'd said. I noted that he was also wearing heels, what we used to call the Cuban lift, boots of mahogany-red leather with a three-inch heel.

Ever since that night, Diana had worn those open-toed shoes perhaps a little more than she ought to. A Brazilian woman must always circulate her shoes – if not her men (although there are good arguments to do that too) to keep things fresh and mysteri-ous – and to keep one's foot, calf, thigh, and hip muscles flexible and attuned to the delicate balance of any surface or step. But it was also hard to ignore a compliment from one of the world's most eligible bachelors and most famous hip hop rap artists on the planet. As a man also up on his toes, he had complimented her on those particular Rainbow Open-Toed Ankle-Strapped Studded Accent High Heels.

Diana even wore those shoes to pick up Isabel from the Emergency Crisis Ward. (This latest suicide attempt a combination of vodka shots and Percocet pills taken on an empty stomach while listening to Ricky Martin on a loop – I will illuminate why later). Then Isabel phoned 911. Sometimes she phoned 911, sometimes she phoned Diana and asked her to phone 911, and sometimes she passed out (always dressed in her law school best and very expensive Valentino cream heels) in the public lobby of the Banco Brazil and once in the Sao Paulo Museum of Art – a public place where security was sure to run to her aid, where it wouldn't be assumed she was merely a junkie or a degenerate from one of the many favelas.

This isn't to suggest Isabel is not serious about suicide. She is serious. Deadly serious, if you can forgive the obvious pun. It's just that Isabel has abandonment issues – deep abandonment issues (which I will illuminate in a moment), and these interfere with her Thanatos drive – her death wish – like a roadblock interferes with a border crosser or a driver under the influence – Isabel wants to kill herself but then runs up against the knowledge that she would be contributing to the cycle of trauma that has led her down this depressive path in the first place.

So Diana picks up Isabel and takes her back to her one-bedroom apartment – giving Isabel her double bed while she sleeps on the couch. Meanwhile, Isabel's two-bedroom condominium (leased after Isabel passed her law exams to anticipate her brilliant prosperous future – one bedroom for her and one for an office of files) remains empty. It is partially funded by Diana to supplement whatever medical benefits money are accrued from the legal firm that originally hired Isabel during her most productive and spectacular manic phase – wherein she closed twenty high-profile commercial legal contracts in the amount of time it usually takes to close six or seven. The top-up comes from Diana because, well, Diana is Isabel's older sister and apparently benefitted longer from parental upbringing – no matter how clueless and neglectful – and that means Diana thinks she has an emotional debt to pay to Isabel that is more binding and more long-term than any student loans or mortgage. Every time Diana tries to bring up the issue of letting go of the apartment and moving in with Diana full-time, or renting a smaller and more modest unit, perhaps in Diana's building, or at the very least putting up her condo on Airbnb and maybe turning a profit during the post-suicidal season – which might be an inspiring "looking on the bright side" kind of solution, Isabel nods and says, "When I'm feeling like myself again. I can't think of any of this right now." She stresses her point by either throwing up or running a fever or becoming completely catatonic and responding to no stimuli whatsoever. Diana has had to give it to Isabel: Isabel was talented and her body came up with lots of ways to keep her taken care of by others – mostly by Diana.

So Diana was ascending to her chiropractor appointment – 30 minutes, where the focus would be on Diana's body instead of Isabel's – when the cables snapped.

Accidents are, by their definition, unpredictable affairs. But let's be honest, to a point. Funnily enough, Diana worried about the elevator in her own rundown building. She was on the 12th floor of a 26-storey building (in reality only 25 since there was no 13th floor), although of course there was also a basement and a parking garage that Diana wouldn't enter because there are no gates on her apartment building and people frequently sleep, have sex, and do drugs there. Isabel sometimes went to the parking garage for a cigarette – but most likely as a tempting of fate to see if someone might kill her and absolve her of the responsibility of doing it herself. The elevator was old and sometimes out-of-order and when the out-of-order sign was removed Diana was even more anxious because whenever the plumbing was fixed in her apartment it inevitably leaked, so she didn't have much faith in repairs in her building. Or repairs in general, if her family was any indication – her mother and her estranged father were broken people – they didn't deny it, in fact they flaunted it like shamelessness is flaunted during Carnival – a gigantic "Hey, we're all fucked up and we're all going to die too soon anyway so we might as well drink and dance and shake all our private parts in the name of Jesus – Christo – because life is a parade that brings you little bursts of magic every so often to seduce you into the daily suffering of your life."

This is why Brazilian women wear high heels, and why when the elevator snapped in the twelve-storey building of Diana's chiropractor she was wearing the very shoes that made her feel she'd attracted a little bit of magic into her otherwise suffering life.

In fact, when the elevator cables – both at once – snapped, Diana was momentarily suspended in the air – like an angel – her feet dangling below her, arms rising as if in a long feathered glorious motion of flight. A flash like celestial lightning appeared before her eyes (it was only afterwards that she understood this was an electrical surge which caused all the numbers on the console to light up at once and then burn out). Strangely enough, Diana thought about her father, Fernando – a man she tried to keep out of her mind as much as possible. He was a hopeless coward who had run away from their mother and started another family with an Amazon woman who spoke no Portuguese. He said it was so they could never argue. When Diana was a very small child, one and two, her father had tossed her like a volleyball into the wide blue endless Brazilian sky.

Up and down.

Up and down.

Like an elevator.

Until the cables of his mind snapped.

It was with a bit of disbelief that Diana – tinged with intense nostalgia confronting a situation that might have ended with her death – oh, how Isabel would have been supremely jealous – was surprised by the force of love hurtling inside her heart during those moments inside and then outside her father's arms. Which was better, she didn't know: leaving his arms to be caressed by the wind, to be for a moment an element safe and miraculous among the elements, or to be caught, warmly and securely from that illusion of eternal protection in the conscious and all-too-human hairy, sweaty, but sturdy arms of her father? She never doubted the sky.

A third floor is tricky in terms of elevators. A third floor is a decision-making floor – should you walk? – not if you are a Brazilian woman in your high-heeled shoes, and if you are a Brazilian woman you are definitely in high-heeled shoes. That is the distinction that absolves you of all responsibility when you decide to take an elevator to floor number 3.

Because there was a basement and two levels of parking garage, Diana's elevator hurtled down somewhere between four and five floors, crashing to a halt on the concrete of the lower parking garage.

I forgot to mention there were two other people in the elevator at the time: a happy accident for one and an unhappy accident for the other.

Happy Accident: Elevator Passenger #1

was on his way to the 12th floor to surprise his girlfriend, who has a psychotherapy practice in the building. Passenger #1 found it exhilarating to date a psychotherapist because he felt she'd be comfortable talking about all kinds of sexual fetishes and desires without judgement. Passenger #1 didn't really have any perverse desires – he liked to dole out a spanking now and then and he wouldn't say no to nipple clamps – but he liked the idea of talking to his psychotherapist girlfriend about sex play. In fact, he was on his way to surprise her with a cock ring he'd purchased in a sex store that was conveniently located across the street from her practice. "Every woman wants a man to give her a ring," the voluptuous dyed-blonde clerk joked as she punched in the price. He was already sporting a hard-on in the elevator when the cables snapped.

Happy Accident because his girlfriend was in the middle of an afternoon tryst with the other psychotherapist in the building – and this man was into being smacked around and whipped. His moans could be heard down the halls of the floor.

A month later, after Passenger #1 had completed the majority of his rehab for a broken hip, he asked his psychotherapist girlfriend to marry him. She agreed and he put a white gold and diamond ring on her finger. The accident had spurred the psychotherapist to take a good look at her life and even though she was an open-minded progressive psychotherapist who didn't mind whipping a man wearing a ball chain inside his mouth she thought God had given her a sign about the sum effect of promiscuity. Besides, she was pregnant, and she wasn't entirely sure who the father was but she knew she didn't want whipping boy involved in the raising of any child of hers. Two psychotherapists were not better than one.

(When they were finally rescued by paramedics, the cock ring – found in the corner of the elevator by Paramedic #2 – elicited a steady supply of laughs and speculations for months to come from a group of people whose days needed a laugh because it mostly consisted of overdoses and projectile vomit and cardiac arrests.)

Unhappy Accident: Elevator Passenger #2

an obese man, he happened to be holding onto the elevator railing when the cables snapped and so his hang time was considerably less than Passenger #1's and Cousin Diana's. He had acted as a kind of cushioning mattress to both – like the rubber corners on a pinball machine (which is ironic because he did enjoy playing pinball – a Beatles-themed pinball game at his local beer pub – the beer of course contributing to his obesity). In fact, when the cable snapped, he'd been humming "I Wanna Hold Your Hand," while thinking about the nachos he was going to order as a treat after seeing his dentist on the 8th floor. He'd been putting off coming in for months because the dentist had ordered a special set of X-rays and Passenger #2 did not want to know the results. The receptionist kept calling. She said they would charge him if he cancelled another appointment. Although the X-rays were clear of anything more serious than gingivitis, Passenger #2 felt the rug of the world getting pulled from under him.

His obesity gave him little balance and he belly-flopped forward making a star on the elevator floor.

Passenger #1 hit the ground two seconds before Cousin Diana and crushed Passenger #2's arm – breaking it in three places – and then he fell backwards onto Passenger #2's legs – breaking them, too, causing a blood clot that would eventually turn into a fatal hemothorax.

Cousin Diana landed on both feet, and for a split second she thought she'd performed the perfect gymnastics dismount – when both ankles snapped.

Diana fell on Passenger #2's spine, which, covered in fat, provided Diana with a cushion not unlike the blue gymnasium mats she remembered jumping onto as a child. Diana sometimes had dreams of her sister Isabel jumping off buildings and bridges – even though jumping was not Isabel's preferred suicidal ideation – to be saved by one such blue gym mat. Diana bounced back up and then back down on Passenger #2's spine.

(The cock ring had, at first, also landed on Passenger #2's spine, but Diana's bouncing caused it to roll over Passenger #2's shoulder and into a corner. To add insult to injury, the dentist would send Passenger #2 an invoice for his missed appointment while he was still an in-patient at the hospital.)

You hear about people, perfect strangers, who suddenly find themselves in a dangerous or traumatic or life-threatening situation – who end up bonding with each other, confessing secrets they've never shared, not even with a sibling or a psychotherapist – keeping in touch and sharing special psychic wounds for the rest of the their lives.

You hear about it but then you don't really meet these people so you doubt it.

After the paramedics lifted Diana onto a stretcher – her Rainbow Open-Toed Ankle-Strapped Studded Accent High Heels miraculously intact with her ankles caved in the opposite direction – she never had another thought about Passenger #1 or Passenger #2 – the female paramedic who gave her an IV – "we have to give everyone an IV out of principle" – had said, "those are the most fabulous shoes I've ever seen – where did you get them?"

Diana wasn't in the habit of lying. When your sister is openly suicidal and your father has abandoned your family, conversations about all kinds of things that other people would consider touchy or inappropriate don't faze you and Diana didn't need to lie to save face. Maybe it was the shock of it all. But Diana replied that a famous rapper had given them to her as a gift. "You know _____?" Diana nodded with flirtatious pride. "I work for him. He's a true gentleman. And has a great eye for shoes."

Diana then passed out. While she passed out the paramedic – who would usually start sexting with her boyfriend who refused to commit until Brazil won another Gold in Men's soccer at the World Cup – every night she asked Mother Mary not only to help the Men's Soccer team to reach Olympic Gold Victory but to change the World Cup format to every year instead of every four years so she could bear the three children she'd always dreamed of having – took out several packs of alcohol swabs and gave Diana's shoes a thorough wipe, almost as if they were babies of her own and she was caressing every bit of their flesh with her mother's love.

Now, I think it's a good time to bring up mothers. Diana and Isabel's mother was all too present, especially when Isabel was in the hospital. Their mother would show up dressed to the nines, like it was a fancy nightclub for senior citizens (and there are a number of these in Brazil, located in shopping malls and underused churches). Their mother, Maria, who because of her name liked to imagine all prayers were directed at her, couldn't bear to pass up an opportunity to curse their father in front of witnesses, and a daughter with serious abandonment issues on a carousel of suicide attempts fit the bill. She set up shop, so to speak, outside Isabel's room – not inside where she might actually be called upon to help with a sponge bath or open Isabel's meal tray or even just to listen to why Isabel thought that once again life wasn't worth living – but outside Isabel's room in a comfy leather chair she'd dragged from the nurses' lounge (you can basically do what you want in a hospital if you are the mother of a suicidal daughter) so she could accost any psychiatrist, nurse, social worker, physiotherapist, janitor, or visitor of any other patient and regale them with her litany of woes. "If life is a series of ups and downs, I wonder where all my ups disappeared to."

As soon as Isabel started to get a bit of colour in her cheeks, asking for an extra yogurt at breakfast, Mother Maria packed up shop – abandoning her leather chair for staff to drag back into the nurses' lounge, decamping the hospital before the discharge papers were signed, leaving Diana to transfer Isabel to her apartment.

Mother Maria refused to take Isabel in and refused to help Diana out financially. "When do I get to enjoy life?" she'd say, although Diana knew she barely left her own condo – a three-bedroom paid for by her inheritance – watching soap operas for most of the day and ordering in a different take-out menu every night. She'd claimed that her openness to all kinds of cuisine constituted her case for being well-travelled.

Diana knew it was a cruel thought – though thoroughly warranted and fair – that her mother was simply enjoying life as she held court (oh to be judge and jury!) outside Isabel's hospital room.

But when Diana of the Broken Ankles was taken to hospital, Mother Maria made only a brief appearance, since broken ankles and possible concussion would probably amount to just one night in hospital – Mother Maria didn't think it was worth dressing up for, or dragging a chair from the nurses' lounge. What kind of suffering could she claim in such a short-term situation? After all, Diana had clearly been involved in an accident – and considering the serious injuries of Unhappy Accident Passenger #2 – had come out unscathed. What could she say, except, "You teach your children to take precautions using elevators and they just ignore you." It didn't hold the gravitas she'd grown accustomed to and, anyway, everyone used elevators nowadays. And how could anyone tell if an elevator was precarious? This one was in a reputable building with doctors' offices. No, the only tack she could take was: "Isn't life merely an unjust and scary series of accidents?" Which wasn't exactly crowd compelling.

So Mother Maria barely stayed fifteen minutes, peeking twice into Diana's cramped room (they don't worry about lumping those with broken bones together, it's the broken minds they give space to: as has been noted frequently, when you put too many broken minds in the same room a domino effect occurs and sooner or later they're all crying or screaming or rending their gar-

ments or throwing rolled-up magazines at each other's heads) –
first, to see if there was perhaps an extra fold-out chair she could
commandeer for the hall (there wasn't), and second, to ask her
whatever question might have popped into her mind at the
moment. (Strangely enough, this didn't give Diana any abandonment issues. She was grateful to be abandoned, both by her father
and by her mother. She knew Isabel didn't intend to abandon her
either so even though their sisterhood was blatantly one-sided, at
least Diana was on the side that included holding a job and main-
taining an even-keel emotional life – rather rare for a Brazilian.)

When Diana pointed to the freshly polished pair of Rainbow
Open-Toed Ankle-Strapped Studded Accent High Heels, Mother
Maria sighed and clasped her hands together. "Now those are
shoes you wouldn't be embarrassed to die in." Then, "Keep them
away from Isabel."

Yes, it was true. And it was like the shoes knew it. Each nurse
and X-ray technician and cafeteria worker commented on the
radiant beauty of her Rainbow Open-Toed Ankle-Strapped
Studded Accent High Heels. And each time she told them that a
famous rapper had given them to her. It was like she was a
celebrity by proxy; normally a shy and fairly reclusive practical
girl, she took giddy pleasure in this.

"And there's not a scratch on them," she assured. To which the
head nurse replied, "It's a miracle."

You might think this is hyperbole, but all that tells me is
you've never met a Brazilian woman. Or a true Brazilian woman
who hasn't had her fashionista instincts repressed by North
American androgynous dullness.

So it was with utter horror that the verdict came down (and not
by Mother Mary but by the Devil in a white lab coat with a
stethoscope around his neck):

"You will never walk in high heels again."

Of course he said other things before and after this: "You mustn't put weight on your ankles for two months. Then you must only wear slippers and walk for five minute intervals. These are strong painkillers and you don't want to get addicted to them. You will need someone to help you around the house. Who is taking you home?"

But all Diana heard was: "You will never walk in high heels again."

It was as if he had said, "Give up on ever getting married or living a normal life. Your life is now essentially over."

If you think Diana was being overly dramatic or that I am greatly exaggerating, then you've never met a Brazilian let alone a Brazilian woman. And that's a shame. It's always a good thing to have one's priorities shaken up now and then and knowing a Brazilian, particularly a Brazilian woman, will do that for you. Time and time again. Trust me. My mother is Brazilian. But we're not talking about her right now. We're talking about my Cousin Diana, who didn't have anyone to take her home because her mother had already decided this wasn't the right audience for her and had gone off to the shopping mall to stock up on chocolate Easter eggs (Brazilian women experience panic when they see stores with specific items like Easter eggs hanging from the ceiling, feeling that such abundance will only be momentary, and so they need to hoard things like Easter eggs for weeks before the actual holiday), and Isabel, well, Isabel's driver's licence had expired and no doctor would sign off on her getting behind a vehicle, given her long history of suicidal ideation. And even if she had a licence and could drive without thoughts of weaving into the wrong lane, Diana knew any visit to a hospital for a purpose other than to take care of Isabel might make her feel like the one stable thing in her life could no longer be counted on. Aside from Diana, of course.

Now, you might think that Diana was worried about changing lanes, or not, and she was, but she was much more worried about the prospect of a high-heel-less existence. The nurse who had called her unscathed Rainbow Open-Toed Ankle-Strapped Studded Accent High Heels a miracle placed the holy objects on Diana's lap and personally wheeled her down to the taxi stand. Then, at her condo, the taxi driver lifted her from the back seat like a melancholy bride and placed her on the fold-out wheelchair that was hers on loan for the two months, after which she was expected to move to a walker, and then to crutches, and then to slippers, and then, to what? Loafers? Trainers?

As the elevator rose to her condo floor, Diana cursed elevators (except this one – "please don't break down or I don't know what I'll do"): the thought of going out hobbling in Crocs – those were for obese Americans only – was the first time Diana felt she might have to guard against suicidal ideation herself. She was sobbing uncontrollably by the time she buzzed the ringer on her own apartment, calling on Isabel to extract herself from an oasis of pillows and murder mystery novels (people obsessed with their own deaths find other people's murders comforting) to answer the door.

This took several buzzes. Eventually Isabel could be heard shuffling to the door. "Is that you, Diana? Why are you crying? Where's your key?"

Diana was able to stifle her sobs long enough to explain: "The doctor said I'll never walk in high heels again!"

"Doctors don't know a fucking thing, Diana!" Isabel cried, flinging open the door and wheeling Diana in with a force of purpose Diana hadn't seen in almost a decade. "Think of all the bullshit they've said to me over the years."

It was true. Isabel should have suffered massive brain damage – and comas – from all the pills she's taken. She should have heart damage from the pills and panic attacks and nerve damage from the falls and even more brain damage from the concussions. And yet all the tests confirmed Isabel was a perfectly healthy specimen – above average, actually – physically. It was her emotional life that was in a constant state of imbalance and disarray. And no pill or meditation exercise or diet adjustment or talk therapy had really been able to alter what is for her a natural state – in fact, the months of supposed normalcy were when Isabel said she felt unlike herself, halted in some way, like an elevator with an out-of-order sign. Up and down. Up and down. It wasn't an easy way of life, but it was her way of moving in the world.

And Diana's way of moving in the world was on high heels. So during any breaks from her work – that she conducted from a distance on her computer in her living room-now-bedroom plus office plus eating area – Diana committed to proving her doctor wrong.

Isabel placed Diana's miraculous unscathed Rainbow Open-Toed Ankle-Strapped Studded Accent High Heels on the mantle where Diana could easily see them wherever she happened to be in the room. In addition to this place of honour, she also protected the shoes with the cover from their grandmother's crystal dessert platter. The shoes now looked like a holy relic. As they rightfully were.

Diana would stare at the shoes and visualize herself walking in them, skipping in them, even dancing samba in them. She would pray to the shoes to give her the strength to overcome her adversity and be an example to Brazilian women – no, all women, everywhere – how nothing has more power than a woman with her dignity intact – no matter what bullshit the universe throws at you.

Did Diana at any point question whether these acts – in the city of the third largest Art Deco Jesus Statue in the world – were sacrilegious? Not at all. Not even for a millisecond. She knew instinctively Christo would understand. He would approve.

As a side-effect, Isabel too started to pray to the shoes. To grant her the strength to simply walk away – even strut away – from her unhappy thoughts about her childhood abandonment by their father. She even, one evening, laid every single cassette tape, CD, and album of Ricky Martin's "Living la Vida Loca" on the coffee table and asked Diana to throw them all down the garbage compactor (she swore on the shoes she'd also deleted it from her computer and cell phone).

(Oh, I think I forgot to explain, Ricky Martin's "Living la Vida Loca" was a song Isabel used to sing and dance to with her father – one of her only memories of him. Didn't everyone want to be living La Vida Loca? Isabel would torture herself with the song. Every time she ended up in hospital there was evidence of her having listened to it. Afterwards, Isabel always claimed to Diana that she had thrown out the offensive CD or erased the song from her computer but both women knew she was lying. Diana had even phoned Isabel's go-to radio station and begged them to take it off their playlist forever. But everyone loves Ricky Martin's "Living la Vida Loca," they said. "Please, just destroy it and say it was an accident." But they, politely, refused. "We can't control what makes people suicidal just like we can't control what makes people happy. Sad, depressing songs make a lot of people happy. Upbeat party songs send some people to hang from the rafters. It's random. We can't be held responsible.")

But Diana was fighting to hold her chiropractor's building's elevator company responsible. Celebrities weren't the only ones who deserved to have their body parts insured and she wanted the insurance money for the rehab she would need to get past the foldout wheelchair, then walker, then crutches, then slippers, then trainers, then...yes...high heels. She even wrote that in her claim: "Until I am walking comfortably once again in high heels, I will not consider my rehabilitation complete."

Diana and Isabel performed their visualizations at various times of the day and prayed to the shoes at least three times per day (more on weekends). Isabel even suggested they play, as extra motivation, the albums by the famous rapper who had complimented Diana on her shoes. Synergy, she called it. Synergy is very powerful.

The shoes did not let them down. Gradually, Diana abandoned her foldout wheelchair. Then the walker. Then the crutches. (At this point Isabel wanted to have a little party to celebrate but Diana refused, saying they couldn't celebrate until she'd fully reached her goal.) So next she abandoned the slippers, then the trainers, the loafers, the strappy sandals. And then...

Diana slipped her feet into a pair of one-inch high heels, shoes she considered every day walking shoes but which for months had been out of her reach. The pain was excruciating at first, but then she imagined the doctor's agape face as she strutted into the hospital to prove his prognosis wrong, as she bore down and smiled through the indignity like a true Brazilian woman.

Isabel wept as Diana took her first few steps. They even videoed them to send to Mother Maria so she could see what extraordinary daughters she had created out of a worthless man's sperm. (No one ever went so far as to claim Virgin Births in Brazil but it was frequently speculated that Brazilian women possess a unique ability to use a man's sperm for a daughter's conception only – and after that, she would be free of his otherwise incompetent and dysfunctional DNA.)

Isabel was also getting stronger. She no longer lay around all day and had even started to write a murder mystery of her own, called *The Elevator Murders*, about a man who abducted women from elevators and made them prance around in his mother's high heels before killing them. (As it turned out, this would be a Brazilian bestseller and would eventually be made into a Hollywood film starring Ryan Gosling as the killer and Penelope Cruz as his only surviving victim.) She was cooking and cleaning a little and one day after Diana returned from her "training" walk on two-inch heels, Isabel announced, "I'm ready to give up the condo, Diana. That's if you will have me."

Now it was Diana's turn to weep. "Of course, Isabel, if that will make you happy."

"I can't think of anywhere else I'd like to be. You're the only family I need."

And so the sisters hugged and made plans to sell Isabel's condo and they were even getting along (over the phone) with Mother Maria and all of a sudden – after so much hoping and praying – the day had finally come, and Diana and Isabel bowed down in front of the Rainbow Open-Toed Ankle-Strapped Studded Accent High Heels.

They prayed. They prayed longer and with more zeal than they'd ever prayed before.

Isabel lifted the crystal dessert cover. It was as if the room was suddenly bathed in a bright white light. So bright it was hard to look at the shoes head-on. But Diana did and the shoes were as unscathed and luminously polished as when she'd left the hospital.

Diana slipped them on and immediately felt she'd been resurrected.

Isabel couldn't stop jumping up and down. Up and down. "I've never been so happy!" she cheered.

"Neither have I!"

It was while Diana was on her "victory lap" – catwalking the streets of Copacabana and on her way to reveal her glory to the doctor at the hospital that a second accident occurred. This time a happy accident.

Happy Accident Person #1 happened to be Diana herself. Although at first she didn't know it was a happy accident.

A limousine was coming up the street and a mob of women were running – sprinting at breakneck pace – in their high heels towards it. Diana could not cross the street. The limousine halted in front of her, steps away from the now-famous restaurant. Two huge men leapt out – one pushing Diana aside. The mob rammed up against her while the third man – Happy Accident Person #2 – emerged from the limousine! Diana was pressed so hard by the mob of women that she was actually thrown high into the air – just like when she was a little girl – and then she dropped.

During the drop Diana fell into despair, knowing that when she landed on the cobblestones her ankles would re-break and the doctor's prediction of a high-heel-less future would actually materialize. She closed her eyes and gave up, as she imagined Isabel used to do.

But what she felt instead were arms around her waist and then the scooping of her legs and a laying of her head on a large shoulder.

Was she dead? Was this what death was?

She opened her eyes. And there staring into them with a stunned concern was…who could have predicted it? …the famous rapper whose words and music had motivated her all through her elevator ordeal. (So focused had she been on her goal, she hadn't known he was coming to town on a global tour.)

Realizing she was indeed conscious and likely undamaged, he walked briskly towards the restaurant, his two bodyguards on either side, with Diana in his arms. He stopped when he noticed her shoes. A vague memory surfaced – and a deep desire that he had tried his best to repress over the years.

"Those are I-know-who-I-am shoes," Diana whispered into his ear, going completely limp in his arms.

The famous rapper treated Diana to dinner at the heavily guarded restaurant and Diana told him the story of the elevator and what the doctors had told her and how she had listened to his music and prayed to the shoes and had visualized herself dancing in these shoes.

"Well then you must dance in them," he said. "It's a miracle."

He gave her backstage passes to his concert and of course Diana brought Isabel with her and they danced and danced in their high heels until the end of the second encore. (Later, in a strange synergy, it would be the rapper who would produce the Hollywood adaptation of Isabel's murder mystery.)

After the show the rapper took Diana back to his hotel (due to privacy concerns, we must omit the name) and asked if he could remove her shoes and kiss her feet.

Diana could barely believe what was happening. She nodded solemnly and then lay down on the largest and most comfortable bed she'd ever been in, a simple blissful smile on her face. "It's a miracle," she said. And that was before he'd even kissed her feet and her other (some broken, some not) parts.

When she woke it was nearly noon (Diana wasn't used to all the Champagne she'd consumed backstage the night before, nor was she used to such exquisite sheets). She woke with a mild headache but wrapped in a warm cocoon. Yes, it had all happened. She was still in the fancy hotel and her blue dress and silver necklace were hanging over the bedroom suite easy chair. Beside her king-sized feather pillow was a note:

Thank you for falling into my arms.
I will always remember you.
I hope you won't mind –
I helped myself to a souvenir.

He'd taken the Rainbow Open-Toed Ankle-Strapped Studded Accent High Heels! Diana felt a pang of loss, a part of the larger pang she felt at the end of such a glorious happy accident. The shoes had already given her two miracles. Three, if she counted Isabel. It was now fitting that they should find their way onto another person's feet.

And Diana knew exactly how much the rapper wanted those shoes for himself. Brazilian women know themselves, and they know their men – those who are cowards and choose to disappear up the Amazon, and those who willingly follow their desires – sometimes so turbulent that his posse often gives a thumbs-up or a thumbs-down to visitors, letting them know if he is in an up mood or down mood, whether or not they ought to approach.

Clearly, he had returned to his hotel room, telling his bodyguards that he was in a down mood and to not let anyone in – even themselves – and so, while his bodyguards stood outside his suite, Diana's rapper unwrapped the Rainbow Open-Toed Ankle-Strapped Studded Accent High Heels, his heart beating violently, his soul preparing to soar. He'd always had small feet for a man and Diana had largish feet for a woman. There was no question – Diana knew it would be so – that the Rainbow Open-Toed Ankle-Strapped Studded Accent High Heels would be a perfect fit.

She watched him as walk as svelte as a cat up and down his bedroom carpet, knowing he'd never felt such peace, not in his entire turbulent life.

Asking to be given what Diana had already received, she heard him pray to the shoes: "Give me the strength to be who I am."

All we can do now is hope the shoes were able to answer his prayer.

Leanne Milech is a writer and former lawyer living in Toronto. She is now an English professor at Humber College. Leanne's writing has most recently appeared in the *Humber Literary Review* and the *Globe and Mail*. She holds an MFA in Creative Writing from the University of Guelph.

photo by Tyler Bowditch

Edward Brown of Toronto is the author of the short story collection *Playing Basra*. His non-fiction writing includes *On Toronto Train Bridges* and *I Am a Pedestrian* recounting his 159km walk around Toronto's current city limits. He has written extensively about Toronto's early jazz scene. His writing appears in the *Globe and Mail*, *Spacing Magazine* and several other publications.

photo by Ryley Brown

Priscila Uppal had lived in Toronto until her death in 2018. She was a poet, fiction writer, memoirist, essayist, playwright, and a professor of English at York University. Her most recent books were the posthumous collection of poems *On Second Thought* and the anthology *Another Dysfunctional Cancer Poem Anthology*, co-edited with Meaghan Strimas. Among her critically acclaimed publications are ten collections of poetry; the novels *The Divine Economy of Salvation* and *To Whom It May Concern*; the study *We Are What We Mourn: The Contemporary English-Canadian Elegy*; the memoir *Projection: Encounters with My Runaway Mother*; the collection of short stories *Cover Before Striking* and the plays *6 Essential Questions* and *What Linda Said*. Her work has been published internationally and translated into eight languages.

priscilauppal.ca   *photo by Mark Raynes Roberts*

Cara Marks of Victoria, British Columbia, recently completed her Creative Writing Prose Fiction MA with distinction at the University of East Anglia as a recipient of their North American Bursary. Her work has appeared in *Vol. 1 Brooklyn*, *The Nervous Breakdown*, the Commonwealth Writers literary journal *adda* and elsewhere. She writes playful, intimate stories and has been working as Writer-in-Residence at a boarding school just outside of London. She is currently writing her first novel.

William John Wither is a speculative fiction writer living in London, Ontario. He is the lead game designer of *IMPACT: A Foresight Game*, and co-founder of *The C Word*, a fringe card company for the lovingly depraved. He currently works with start-ups in the future-of-food space,

while continuing to write short stories about the future and its many dystopic themes. (You can listen to an audio performance of the story at: tinyurl.com/Wither-42-2)

Mark Paterson of Lorraine, Quebec, is the author of the short story collections *Dreamers and Misfits of Montclair*, *A Finely Tuned Apathy Machine*, and *Other People's Showers*, all from Exile Editions. He is a past winner of the 3Macs carte blanche Prize and *Geist*'s Literal Literary Postcard Story Contest.

markpaterson.ca   *photo by Lynn Brown*

About the Finalists

Lorna Crozier of Vancouver Island, British Columbia, is an Officer of the Order of Canada, and has won several national awards for her poetry, including the Governor General's Award. She has received five honorary doctorates for her contribution to Canadian literature, the most recent from McGill and Simon Fraser. Her first published story was shortlisted for the National Magazine Award in 2017. This is her second.

photo by Ringo Tang

Bruce Meyer is the author or editor of sixty-three books of poetry, short fiction, non-fiction, literary journalism memoirs, and portrait photography. His most recent books are *A Feast of Brief Hopes* (stories) and *The First Taste: New and Selected Poems*. He was the inaugural Poet Laureate of the city of Barrie. He lives in Barrie and teaches at Georgian College and at Victoria College in the University of Toronto. facebook.com/BruceMeyer *photo by Mark Raynes Roberts*

Christine Miscione of Hamilton, Ontario, has appeared in the *This Magazine, Lemon Hound, EXILE/ELQ*, and *The Puritan*. In 2012, her story "Skin, Just" won the Gloria Vanderbilt/Exile CVC Short Fiction Award. In 2014, her debut collection, *Auxiliary Skins*, won the ReLit Award for short fiction. More recently, she placed third in fiction contests organized by *PRISM International, Prairie Fire*, and *The Antigonish Review*, and was shortlisted for the 2018 KM Hunter Award for Fiction. Christine is currently at work on both a novel and a short fiction collection. christinemiscione.com

photo by Mark Tearle

Martha Bátiz was born and raised in Mexico City, but has been living in Toronto since 2003. Her articles, chronicles, reviews and short stories have appeared in newspapers and magazines in her homeland and internationally. She holds a PhD in Latin American Literature, is an instructor of Creative Writing at the University of Toronto, and is a part-time professor at York University/Glendon College. Her most recent books are the Latino Awards-winning collection of stories *Plaza Requiem* (2017), and the novella *Damiana's Reprieve* (2018). She lives in Richmond Hill, Ontario.

marthabatiz.com   @mbatiz   *photo by Emily Ding*
facebook.com/MarthaBatizWriterAndTranslator

Andrea Bradley is a writer, college professor, and recovering lawyer. She has published short stories in several speculative fiction anthologies and magazines. She lives with her family in Oakville, Ontario.   andreabradley.ca   @amcbradley1

CVC8:

Leanne Milech – "The Light in the Closet"
    (winner, Emerging Writer – Toronto, Ontario)
Edward Brown – "Remember Me"
    (co-winner, Any Career Point Writer – Toronto, Ontario)
Priscila Uppal – "Elevator Shoes"
    (co-winner, Any Career Point Writer – Toronto, Ontario)

• Shortlisted:
Cara Marks– "Aurora Borealis"
    (Victoria, British Columbia)
William John Wither – "The Bulbous It with No Eyelids"
    (London, Ontario)
Mark Paterson – "My Uncle, My Barbecue Chicken Deliveryman"
    (Lorraine, Quebec)
Lorna Crozier – "Rebooting Eden"
    (Vancouver Island, British Columbia)
Bruce Meyer – "Cantique de Jean Racine"
    (Barrie, Ontario)
Christine Miscione – "Your Failing Heart."
    (Hamilton, Ontario)
Martha Bátiz – "Suspended"
    (Richmond Hill, Ontario)
Andrea Bradley – "No One Is Watching"
    (Oakville, Ontario)

CVC7:

Halli Villegas – "Road Kill"
    (winner, Emerging Writer – Mount Forest, Ontario)
Seán Virgo – "Sweetie"
    (winner, Any Career Point Writer – Eastend,
Saskatchewan)

• Shortlisted:
Iryn Tushabe – "A Separation"
    (Saskatchewan)
Katherine Fawcett – "The Pull of Old Rat Creek"
    (Squamish, British Columbia)
Darlene Madott – "Winners and Losers"
    (Toronto, Ontario)
Jane Callen – "Grace"
    (Victoria, British Columbia)
Yakos Spiliotopoulos – "Grave Digger"
    (Toronto, Ontario)
Chris Urquhart – "Skinbound"
    (Toronto, Ontario)
Norman Snider – "Husband Material"
    (Toronto, Ontario)
Carly Vandergriendt – "Resurfacing"
    (Montreal, Quebec)
Linda Rogers – "Breaking the Sound Barrier"
    (Victoria, British Columbia)

CVC6:

Matthew Heiti – "For They Were Only Windmills"
    (winner, Emerging; Sudbury, Ontario)
Helen Marshall – "The Gold Leaf Executions"
    (winner, Any Career Point; Sarnia, Ontario/Cambridge, U.K.)

• Shortlisted:
Diana Svennes-Smith – "Stranger In Me"
    (Eastend, Saskatchewan)
Sang Kim – "Kimchi"
    (Toronto, Ontario)
A.L. Bishop – "Hospitality"
    (Niagara Falls, Ontario)
Katherine Govier – "Elegy: Vixen, Swan, Emu"
    (Toronto, Ontario)
Shéila McClarty – "The Diamond Special"
    (Oakbank, Manitoba)
Caitlin Galway – "Bonavere Howl"
    (Toronto, Ontario)
Bruce Meyer – "The Slithy Toves"
    (Barrie, Ontario)
Frank Westcott – "It Was a Dark Day ~ Not a Stormy Night ~
In Tuck-Tea-Tee-Uck-Tuck"
    (Alliston, Ontario)
Martha Bátiz – "Paternity, Revisited"
    (from Mexico; lives Richmond Hill, Ontario)
Leon Rooke – "Open the Door"
    (Toronto, Ontario)
Norman Snider – "How Do You Like Me Now?"
    (Toronto, Ontario)

CVC5:

Lisa Foad – "How To Feel Good"
     (winner, Emerging; Toronto, Ontario)
Nicholas Ruddock – "Mario Vargas Llosa"
     (winner, Any Career Point; Guelph, Ontario)

• Shortlisted:
Hugh Graham – "After Me"
     (Toronto, Ontario)
Josip Novakovich – "Dunavski Pirat"
     (from Croatia; lives Montreal, Quebec)
Leon Rooke – "Sara Mago et al"
     (Toronto, Ontario)
Jane Eaton Hamilton – "The Night SS Sloan Undid His Shirt"
     (Vancouver, British Columbia)
Bruce Meyer – "Tilting"
     (Barrie, Ontario)
Priscila Uppal – "Bed Rail Entrapment Risk Notification Guide"
     (Toronto, Ontario)
Christine Miscione – "Spring"
     (Hamilton, Ontario)
Veronica Gaylie – "Tom, Dick, and Harry"
     (Vancouver, British Columbia)
Maggie Dwyer – "Chihuahua"
     (Commanda, Ontario)
Bart Campbell – "Slim and The Hangman"
     (Vancouver, British Columbia)
Linda Rogers – "Raging Breath and Furious Mothers"
     (Victoria, British Columbia)
Lisa Pike – "Stellas"
     (Windsor, Ontario)

CVC4:

Jason Timermanis – "Appetite"
    (winner, Emerging; Toronto, Ontario)
Hugh Graham – "The Man"
    (winner, Any Career Point; Toronto, Ontario)

• Shortlisted:
Helen Marshall – "The Zhanell Adler Brass Spyglass"
    (Sarnia, Ontario)
K'ari Fisher – "Saddle Up!"
    (Burns Lake, British Columbia)
Linda Rogers – "Three Strikes"
    (Victoria, British Columbia)
Susan P. Redmayne – "Baptized"
    (Oakville, Ontario)
Matthew R. Loney – "The Pigeons of Peshawar"
    (Toronto, Ontario)
Erin Soros – "Morning is Vertical"
    (Vancouver, British Columbia)
Gregory Betts – "Planck"
    (St. Catharines, Ontario)
George McWhirter – "Sisters in Spades"
    (Vancouver, British Columbia)
Madeline Sonik – "Punctures"
    (Victoria, British Columbia)
Leon Rooke – "Slain By a Madam"
    (Toronto, Ontario)

CVC3:

Sang Kim – "When John Lennon Died"
    (winner, Emerging; Toronto, Ontario)
Priscila Uppal – "Cover Before Striking"
    (co-winner, Any Career Point; Toronto, Ontario)
Austin Clarke – "They Never Told Me"
    (co-winner, Any Career Point; Toronto, Ontario)

• Shortlisted:
George McWhirter – "Tennis"
    (Vancouver, British Columbia)
David Somers – "Punchy Sells Out"
    (Winnipeg, Manitoba)
Leon Rooke – "Conditional Sphere of Everyday Historical Life"
    (Toronto, Ontario)
Helen Marshall – "Lessons in the Raising of Household Objects"
    (Sarnia, Ontario)
Yakos Spiliotopoulos – "Black Sheep"
    (Toronto, Ontario)
Greg Hollingshead – "Mother / Son"
    (Toronto, Ontario)
Matthew R. Loney – "A Fire in the Clearing"
    (Toronto, Ontario)
Rob Peters – "Sam's House"
    (Vancouver, British Columbia)
Liz Windhorst Harmer – "Teaching Strategies"
    (Hamilton, Ontario)

CVC2:

Christine Miscione – "Skin, Just"
 (winner, Emerging; Hamilton, Ontario)
Leon Rooke – "Here Comes Henrietta Armani"
 (co-winner, Any Career Point; Toronto, Ontario)
Seán Virgo – "Gramarye"
 (co-winner, Any Career Point; East End, Saskatchewan)

• Shortlisted:
Kelly Watt – "The Things My Dead Mother Says"
 (Flamborough, Ontario)
Darlene Madott – "Waiting (An Almost Love Story)"
 (Toronto, Ontario)
Linda Rogers – "Darling Boy"
 (Victoria, British Columbia)
Daniel Perry – "Mercy"
 (Toronto, Ontario)
Amy Stuart – "The Roundness"
 (Toronto, Ontario)
Phil Della – "I Did It for You"
 (Vancouver, British Columbia)
Jacqueline Windh – "The Night the Floor Jumped"
 (Vancouver, British Columbia)
Kris Bertin – "Tom Stone and Co."
 (Halifax, Nova Scotia)
Martha Bátiz – "The Last Confession"
 (Richmond Hill, Ontario)

CVC1:

Silvia Moreno-Garcia – "Scales as Pale as Moonlight"
    (co-winner, Emerging; Vancouver, British Columbia)
Frank Westcott – "The Poet"
    (co-winner, Emerging; Shelburne Ontario)
Ken Stange – "The Heart of a Rat"
    (winner, Any Career Point; Toronto, Ontario)

• Shortlisted:
Hugh Graham – "Through the Sky"
    (Toronto, Ontario)
Leigh Nash – "The Field Trip"
    (Toronto, Ontario)
Rishma Dunlop – "Paris"
    (Toronto, Ontario)
Zoe Stikeman – "Single-Celled Amoeba"
    (Toronto, Ontario)
Kristi-ly Green – "The Patient"
    (Toronto, Ontario)
Gregory Betts – "To Tell You"
    (Oakville Ontario)
Richard Van Camp – "On the Wings of This Prayer"
    (Edmonton, Alberta)

Exile's $15,000 Carter V. Cooper Short Fiction Competition

$10,000 for the Best Story by an Emerging Writer

$5,000 for the Best Story by a Writer at Any Career Point

The shortlisted are published in the annual *CVC Short Fiction Anthology Series* and selected writers in *EXILE Quarterly*

Exile's $3,000 Gwendolyn MacEwen Poetry Competition

$1,500 for the Best Suite by an Emerging Writer

$1,500 for the Best Suite of Poetry

Winners are published in *EXILE Quarterly*

These annual competitions run March to September

Details at: www.ExileQuarterly.com

FOR CANADIAN WRITERS ONLY